GHOST OF A FLEA

Other Books by James Sallis

NOVELS

THE LONG-LEGGED FLY
MOTH
BLACK HORNET
EYE OF THE CRICKET
BLUEBOTTLE
DEATH WILL HAVE YOUR EYES
RENDERINGS

STORIES

A FEW LAST WORDS
LIMITS OF THE SENSIBLE WORLD
TIME'S HAMMERS: COLLECTED STORIES

POEMS

SORROW'S KITCHEN
BLACK NIGHT'S GONNA CATCH ME HERE: SELECTED
POEMS, 1968–1998

AS EDITOR

ASH OF STARS: ON THE WRITING OF
SAMUEL R. DELANY
JAZZ GUITARS
THE GUITAR IN JAZZ

OTHER

THE GUITAR PLAYERS
DIFFICULT LIVES
SAINT GLINGLIN BY RAYMOND QUENEAU
(TRANSLATOR)
GENTLY INTO THE LAND OF THE MEATEATERS
CHESTER HIMES: A LIFE

GHOST OF A FLEA

A LEW GRIFFIN NOVEL

James Sallis

Walker & Company ❀ *New York*

First published in the United States of America in 2001 by
Walker Publishing Company, Inc.

Published simultaneously in Canada by Fitzhenry and Whiteside,
Markham, Ontario L3R 4T8

For information about permission to reproduce selections from
this book, write to Permissions, Walker & Company, 435 Hudson Street,
New York, New York 10014

Library of Congress Cataloging-in-Publication Data
Sallis, James, 1944–
Ghost of a flea : a Lew Griffin novel / James Sallis.
p. cm.
ISBN 0-8027-3369-7 (alk. paper)
1. Griffin, Lew (Fictitious character)—Fiction. 2. Private
investigators—Louisiana—New Orleans—Fiction. 3. African American
detectives—Fiction. 4. New Orleans (La.)—Fiction. I. Title.
PS3569.A462 G48 2001
813'.54 21; aa05 06-07—dc01
2001026799

Series design by M. J. DiMassi

Printed in the United States of America

2 4 6 8 10 9 7 5 3 1

To Jane Rector-Donaldson
Rich and Abi Martin
Emily and Joe Ferri

My beautiful ship O my memory
Have we sailed far enough
In waters bad to drink
Have we sailed far enough
From the beautiful dawn to the sad
evening!

—APOLLINAIRE

GHOST OF A FLEA

1

AFTER a while I got up and walked to the window. I felt that if I didn't say anything, if I didn't think about what had happened, didn't acknowledge it, somehow it might all be all right again. I listened to the sound of my feet on the floor, the sounds of cars and delivery vans outside, my own breath. Whatever feelings I had, had been squeezed from me. I was empty as a shoe. Empty as the body on the bed behind me.

A limb bowed and pecked at the window, bowed and pecked again. Winds were coming in across Lake Ponchartrain with pullcarts of rain in their wake. I heard music from far off but couldn't tell what it was, not even what kind. Maybe only wind caught in the building's hard throats and hollows, or the city's random noise congealing.

I seem never to learn that standing still doesn't work. There you are with a smile on your face, *they won't notice me*, and all the while all the things you fear keep moving towards you, their smiles a violent travesty of your own. "In your books you never write about anything that's not past, done with, gone," La-Verne had said years ago. She knew that was a way to stand still, too. And she'd been right—about that as about so much else.

Sooner or later I'd have to move. Go back out there, into the world, a world much smaller now, where it was about to rain. And where one of the coldest winters in New Orleans history like a bit player waited impatiently in the wings, strutting and thrumming, for its cue to go on.

I'd spent my life in rooms much like this. You move, like a hermit crab, into their shell. Then in time, as old clothes and mattresses do, they begin taking on your form. Their safe, familiar walls are a second skin. You and the room become of a size and kind, indistinguishable. The room, its surfaces, its volumes, diminish when you leave; and you in turn, away from the room too long, find yourself growing restless, edgy, at loose ends.

I peered out the window, a dim image of the room behind me superimposed there like a fading photograph or one taken too soon from the developing tray, suspended half-formed, neither wholly out of the world nor quite a part of it. The window had become a universal mirror. In it everything was reversed, turned about, transformed: light bled away to darkness, walls and corners bent to obscure, indecipherable shapes, the whole of the room lumpen, autumnal.

And out there in the window-world where a moth beat against glass, a man I knew both too well and not at all stood watching. A man dark and ill-defined, with the mark of lateness, of the autumnal, upon him too.

I remembered Henry James's remark upon meeting George Gissing that he appeared to be a man "quite particularly marked out for what is called in his and my profession an unhappy ending." Gissing had deployed his creativity as the single dynamic force in a life otherwise marked by doubts and indecision, discord, disappointment, disillusion. All of which had a familiar ring to it.

I must come to some sort of conclusion, I suppose, I had written, years ago. *I can't imagine what it should be.* Now I knew.

All the people we've met, all those memories and voices real or imagined, the hoarse whisper of our communal sadness, the beat of regret and sorrow in our blood, the haphazard apprehensions that have made us what we are—they're out there now in the darkness, all of them, at these silent barricades. All the people (as LaVerne used to say) we've watched disappear out the back windows of trains. LaVerne, parents, Hosie Straughter, Vicky, Baby Boy McTell. Myself. This odd man Lew Griffin who understood so much about others and so little, finally, about himself.

Another moth joins the first. Together, apart, they beat soundlessly at the window's periphery. This late-comer, a sphinx moth, has the body of a bulldog, colors like those of an oil slick in moonlight. Also called a hawkmoth. I watch the two familial insects, who could scarcely be more dissimilar, bump and bounce away from the window, skitter the length of its glass in long slides. Perhaps I should value my life more, that something else so badly wants in.

Because the volume has been increased, or because other sounds have fallen away, I can make out the music now. Charlie Patton's slurred voice and guitar, like hands that have gone into water and come out with something shapeless, something that nonetheless coheres for just a moment before it begins spilling away. *Po' Boy, Long Way from Home.*

A long way indeed.

Here in this still room, then, in this moment before the world returns in a rush and bears me back into it, I will tell you what I know: It is not yet midnight. It is not yet raining.

2

ALOUETTE named the child for her mother. She was born on Epiphany, January 6, and I first saw her two hours later at Touro Infirmary, her father standing alongside grinning. Larson was a good, uncomplicated, immensely kind man.

"'ew," he said when I stepped into the room, his *L* an unvoiced breath. I'd never been able to decide if he had an impediment or if that *L* with the tongue's trip from the top of the mouth down was just too much effort for him. I was 'ew, his wife was 'ette. Not that he said much any other time, either. Scientists claim that in our lifetime we spend a total of twelve years talking. If there's any kind of sliding scale, Larson would live to an advanced age.

We shook hands. His was rough and scarred, bleached in patches to a whitish, puttylike gray, elsewhere stained darker, by the cleansers and chemicals he used in his work. Larson restored old buildings. One of the few times I'd heard full sentences from him was a year or so past when we'd sat out on the porch after dinner sharing a beer and he began talking about a house he was working on. You wouldn't believe what-all these old places have wrong with them, he said. Everything on God's earth looks to be out to destroy them. Termites like you've never seen. Mold and rot everywhere. Ground settles, trying to crack them open, and when that doesn't work it moves off somewhere else and settles again. People rip out their insides. Wonder any of them manage to go on standing. But they do.

I stood there by Alouette and the baby, grinning myself, remembering once years ago walking up Magazine watching people as they made their way out of the business district by car, bus, foot and streetcar. I'd been thinking then about the homes, families, meals and easy chairs they were headed back to, thinking how that world flowing past was one I'd never know. Alouette's mother told me that the two of us were just alike, that we'd never find anyone permanent, anyone who'd go the long haul, who cared that much.

All that was a long time ago.

Early morning light spilled through the window onto us. Alouette was asleep. It was as though time were suspended, as though the very morning held its breath. Day became a squirrel gliding between trees in a long, silent jump.

"They're both okay, the nurses said."

Larson nodded.

"Tell her I was here? I'll call or come back by later."

Another nod.

"Let me know if you need anything."

"Y'bet."

But when I stepped out, Larson followed. We stood by a hall window. Below in the street a Toyota had tried to make it past a turning eighteen-wheeler carrying plumbing fixtures and had wound up lodged underneath. We watched firemen's efforts to extricate the Toyota's driver. A team from the hospital hovered about a gurney at crowd's edge, hugging themselves against the cold, waiting. Lights from police and emergency vehicles lashed the street.

"She tell you about the notes?" Larson asked.

I shook my head.

"Think she meant to. *Hope* she did. Else I'm 'bout to step in it here. Pull you along."

When his eyes cut towards mine, I said: "At work, you mean." Alouette was a community activist. Rattling cages, shaking jars that had sat too long unmolested on shelves and getting in people's faces was what she did, what she was good at. People got upset. They were supposed to. Sometimes abrasiveness hauled in results on its back. Sometimes it didn't. Sometimes results not intended hopped aboard and made the trip.

Larson allowed as how it had been, yes, at work.

"Threats."

He nodded.

"Anything specific?"

"Not really. Impression I got, she was supposed to know already."

"Did she?"

Larson shrugged. "Have to ask 'ette."

"You have any idea what the threats were about? Who they might have been from?"

No.

We stood together looking down at the revolving lights, circle of medical deacons about the car.

"Case she was working on, maybe," Alouette being still, between bouts of raising ideological hell, a caseworker.

"Could be." He shrugged. "You know how 'ette is. Save the world. Dozen or more balls in the air. No way she's gonna keep them all up there. Sooner or later they start comin' down on folks's heads."

"But she took the threats seriously?"

"She told me about them. So I have to figure she must of."

Down in the street they dragged the driver from the Toyota. We watched as head and trunk came free, a young woman wearing a blue blazer, light blue shirt, red tie. Her legs hung oddly, like a doll's. As did her head.

"I'll need to see her files. What she was working on, correspondence, any notebooks or the like."

"Most a that's up to the Center. Have to ask them there. Not my world." Larson spread fingers wide on the sill. I thought of the wingspan of large birds: eagles, hawks. Just before those splayed, discolored fingers fell lightly onto my arm.

I was sitting in Joe's, heading for a record. I'd come in early yesterday afternoon for a coffee and never left. A regular named Jimmy and I had been talking and got to wondering how long anyone ever sat in a bar without drinking. Now, though I didn't know whether momentum or inertia would be the appropriate term, I was too far invested in the thing to get up and go. Here I was. Too much coffee had my nerve ends flapping like tatters of flags left behind once all the Pattons, Westmorelands and Schwarzkopfs have had their way, dark things were beginning to move in the corners whenever I looked away, and I'd had enough weird conversations to last well into the next century. But here I was.

Not the original Joe's, of course. That sad, used-up old place had passed during the Seventies. Briefly there'd been an uptown, unreasonable facsimile, someone's halfhearted attempt at resuscitation, body pronounced DOA. But locals had kept the memory alive, till finally a new crop of moneyed folk thought to kick the tired horse to its feet one more time. Joe's had come back as, essentially, a theme park, nostalgia island.

"Have to say I'm surprised you suggested meeting here." Don stared at the cheeseburger they'd set down before him. Then his eyes crossed to the beer glass. A stanchion he could trust. "Authenticity be damned, huh? Glitz! Glamour! New Orleans' answer to the new Times Square."

"Tradition."

"Tradition. Right. Ain't what it used to be," he said.

"What is?"

"Not burgers, obviously." He lifted the bun to look underneath. "You have any idea what these things might be that're growing on here?" With one finger he winnowed out a mushroom. It looked like those I'd once found sprouting from my welcome mat following a hard hour's rain and a day or so of sun.

"Cremini mushrooms."

He'd made a nice pile of them by then.

"First cousin to athlete's foot and people pay good money—"

"Damn good money."

"—to eat them."

I shrugged. "White folk, Massuh Don. What can I say?"

His head wagged sideways two or three times, incredulous. Then he started stoking in demushroomed burger. Swallows of beer followed each bite.

"So," I said. "How you filling your days now?"

"It's only been three."

"You don't work it from the first, they get longer."

"Thought I might take to reading some of those books you're always going on about."

"Good thought."

"Or then again, maybe I'll just get in the habit of hanging around making a full-time pain in the ass of myself, like you."

"Someone came to me and asked, like for a rec-
ommendation, I'd have to tell them you're not half
bad at it. Being a pain in the ass, I mean. Definitely
some nachural talent there. Even if being a cop's what
you're good at."

"Fact is, that's *all* I was ever good at. Never much
going for me with the family thing, for instance."

"Not what I meant."

"I know."

Thirty, forty years Don held the reins on New Orleans' criminal element, and he'd done as good a job
at it as anyone would ever do. Five years ago his son
killed himself. There'd been a bad patch then. For a
while Don had moved in with me, going through mo-
tions, he said, hoping if he just kept on, somehow,
someday, it'd all start making sense again. Then three
years ago, walking into a print shop to have copies
made of insurance forms, he'd met Jeanette.

He finished the burger and last swallow of beer.
"We've done our turn on the floor, Lew, you and me."

"More ways than one."

"For sure." Don laughed. "You especially."

"But you probably meant dancing—as a metaphor."

"Of course I did. Absolutely. A metaphor." He
pushed away his plate and signaled for another beer.

"And now all your dances are gonna be with
Jeanette."

He looked away and back. "Don't I hope."

By ten that night, a few hours after Don walked aslant
and slightly weaving out the door, I decided to head
home myself. That wasn't good enough for a record,
the hell with it. Made it erect out the front door, surprising enough in light of all those hours of sitting
and all the years stacked up behind me, and watched

the storm go from dog paddle to channel swimmer as I walked home. Gentlemanly palms along St. Charles bowed deeply. In yards off Prytania, banana trees were bent almost horizontal, their fan-blade leaves spread in layers close to the ground, like canopies over tiny rain forests. Driven by wind, first at my ankles, then at midcalf, debris ran about me in a stream: Popeye's containers, plastic cups resembling the half-crushed, emptied-out shells of insects, burrito wrappers, cigarette packets, bits of bird's nest, chunks of foam insulation like weightless cheese, part of a yard flamingo, tennis balls, sheet after sheet of notebook paper and one of gold-foil gift wrap, half a loaf of French bread hollowed into a canoe.

A group of children rode by on a motley of bikes. They stood on pedals and leaned hard against the wind at each stroke, dipping deeply to one side then the other. Feral with both youth and the release of the storm, with a kind of permission it gave them, they shouted back and forth at the top of their voices. A police helicopter thwacked by overhead, spotlight a bright, impersonal finger prodding at houses, streets, trees and cars.

Pushed back into the narrow crawl space between two apartment buildings, a young man wrapped in plastic bags secured with spirals of heavy twine sat holding a small dog. Dog's eyes and man's eyes alike anxiously swept the sky.

I got as far as the bench inside the front door, having forgotten to lock the latter again, which was just as well since I'd also forgotten to bring keys, before collapsing. No one home by the look and sound of things. Light from streetlamps came through low-set windows tall as a man. As though in contrast to the fury building outside, light fell gently onto the floor, emphasizing the slope and roll of it, drawing attention to every warped board, every swollen joining. I sat thinking how wood long ago brought down, carved to dull lumber and laid in place, still remembered roundness as a tree and tried to find its way back.

Then I sat not thinking at all.

Hours later, still on the bench, I woke to a world transformed. Leaves and limbs had been stripped from trees, causing them to look skeletal, asymmetrical, incomplete, like some new species struggling through to existence. Strata of topsoil, too, had been peeled away, laying open alluvial years. Elsewhere drifts of sand, rubbish and silt, aleatory dunes, sat a foot or more in height. With bare hands you could dig down to 1990 or 1964, plot out the lives of those who lived then, dredge up flatware, trinkets, seamed nylons. Gutters and streetside had become harbors clogged with ships: colored glass bottles, hundreds of them, washed up from who knows what primal deposits, Log Cabin, Vicks VapoRub, Bromo-Seltzer, Hadacol, Dr. Tichenor's, startling both in their colors and long-forgotten familiarity. Sea-washed, bright and smooth, they clanked and rang and cast off flares of blue, amber, green. I sat thrown into the past myself by the sight of all those bottles, by the flood of memory and sensation they brought on, wholly unaware for the moment of the message lying coiled like a serpent in my answering machine.

3

'D been here a year, year and a half, when I first came across him. The city was full of eccentrics and never shut them away like they did back home—actually took pride in them, in fact. Preacher, the Duck Lady, Doo-Wop.

Nineteen or so, strolling innocently along, I glanced into an alleyway as I passed and saw a man kneeling there. Elbows climbed into light and sank. "That's it, you're doing fine," the man said. "Push, push. You're almost there, Patrice . . ."

Intrigued, I walked closer. No one else in the alley with him, though arms and hands worked steadily as he dipped and straightened, smiled, frowned with concentration. Under his breath, a subterranean river, ran a steady murmur of numbers, Latin, self-interrogation, misgivings, encouragement.

"Are you okay, sir?"

His face came around quickly, like a cat's.

"What, four years of college, four more of medical

school, not to mention internship and residency, you think I can't handle this?

"Push. *Push*, Patrice.

"Well, boy, don't just stand there," he told me. Sweat poured off him; he trembled. "Get over here and take this baby while I see to the mother." The two of us alone in the alley.

Doc's been around for years, a bartender told me later that day. He'd pop up, trek all over the city delivering make-believe babies in alleyways and vacant lots—duplicating the very scene I'd just witnessed—then drop out of sight. No one knew where he lived, or anything about him.

"Weird," I said.

"I guess. You want another?" When he brought it, he said, "Guess you're new in town, huh?"

4

No ONE knows anything about him," Deborah said. I'd mentioned that it was one of those names we all recognized, even if we didn't know much else; maybe the titles of a play or two, or some half-baked notion of *Lysistrata*'s plot. "He lived to be about sixty. As early as his twenties, he'd grown bald. He served as a councillor of some sort, had a couple of sons, won six first prizes for his plays and four seconds. That's about it."

"Not many playwrights have that long a career."

Deborah laughed. "Most of us don't have a career at all."

I'd made a fresh pot of coffee, and put a cup on the table in front of her.

"Thanks, Lew. Smells wonderful."

"Medicinal."

"Always."

A script of the play, blown up on a copier for easier reading and to make room for Deborah's notes, sat there too. Alternate translations ran in green cursive above some lines. Stage directions and blocking were printed in red at the left margin, miscellaneous notes and self-queries penciled in a scrawl at the right. Highlighted in yellow on one page I saw:

> At present I am not my own master; I am very young and am watched very closely. My dear son never lets me out of his sight; he's an unbearable creature, who would quarter a thread and skin a flint; he is afraid I should get lost, for I am his only father.

In the margin Deborah had written *son dresses father in fashionable new tunic—Persian,* and I remembered Emerson, *Beware of enterprises that require new clothes.*

"The beginning should work great. One of the slaves watching over the old man tells us what the play will be like, but he's lying the whole time. I just have to find a way to bring this out."

"Well," I said, "definitely time for a revival, at any rate."

Revival was what she'd taken to calling her staging of the ancient play, grinning like some Hollywood shark given three minutes to pitch his spiel.

"Resuscitation is more like it," I'd responded the first time she came up with that. Then: "The thing could do with a zippier title, too, while you're at it. *Return of the Wasps,* maybe."

"*Son of Wasps.*"

"Or jack it up a whole other notch, go for the grabber: *Sting!*"

"That's it! With the exclamation point a stinger!"

"And a drop of blood at the tip."

We laughed and poured more of the wine she brought home to celebrate. Lifting my glass in a toast, I said, "Happy you're getting the chance to do this." The grant came jointly through Tulane's drama department and a loose association of several local arts foundations. She'd learned of it from one of her regular customers at the flower shop, a cardiologist on the board of a couple of those foundations, and had applied more or less on whim.

"Me too. I thought . . . well, I guess I thought the theater thing was all over, that I'd had whatever chance I was likely to get."

"No second acts in American lives?"

"Something like that."

I sat down beside her now as I had then.

"Thanks, Lew." She stared for a moment at the script. Commentary and notes had begun not to change the play in any elemental manner but subtly to reshape it, urging plot, surround, self and minions toward—what? She didn't know. That's what she was searching for. "Hellacious amount of work hiding in the woodpile."

"And one hell of a woodpile. But it just so happens we're running a special on homilies this week, Ms. O'Neil. Two for one." Made as though to rummage in a bag, see what we had left. "Got Anything worth doing, If it was easy, Hang tough. Few more in there, looks like." I leaned close. "Just between the two of us, marking them down's the only way we've found to move this stuff off the shelves."

"Like what Bierce said about good advice."

"Right. Only thing you can do with it's give it to someone else—fast."

She was, as usual, wearing a long, full skirt, and when she leaned back, drawing legs under, the skirt took away not only her legs but the chair's as well, along with a good few inches of floor.

A group of young people went by laughing and from the sound of it doing their version of dirty dozens on the street outside.

"That's something else I never thought I'd have,

Lew. Couldn't imagine ever being close enough to someone long enough to have private jokes, places, thoughts that didn't need to be completed, stories all our own. I love having that, Lew."

"I do too."

We sat there quietly a moment.

"I could fix more coffee," I said.

"Two pots are enough—even for New Orleanians."

She leaned forward to turn on the radio, found some small-combo jazz, Dolphyesque baritone sax weaving a floor for guitar and piano to walk on. Then a soprano sax sounding scarily like Sidney Bechet started up. Another New Orleans boy like Louis Armstrong and with him one of the truly great jazz soloists. They'd always said Bechet was so good you could put him in front of an army band and he'd even swing *that*. Bechet, who'd play great music anytime, anywhere, but would never consent to play nigger, and went off to Paris to live instead.

I turned back from the window to find Deborah's eyes bright. She'd been watching me.

"You miss it."

"What?"

"All of it. The books. What you used to do out on the streets, helping people. Teaching. LaVerne and Clare."

"A curious list." I smiled. "And a long time ago."

"No. It wasn't, Lew. Not long at all. That's my point."

"It's just . . ."

"Just?"

"I have a family now. You, David, Alouette and her crew. Maybe not exactly the kind of family Republicans are always going on about, but a family nonetheless. Things change."

"Things do, yes. I'm not sure people do."

I picked up our cups and took them to the sink. Stood there a moment looking out the window. Bat,

Clare's cat, now mine, jumped onto the windowsill out-side and began rubbing shoulder and head against it.

"I don't think I can explain it, or even that I un-derstand it myself. But it's a little like when you're crossing the lake." The bridge over Lake Ponchartrain was twenty-five miles long. "You get halfway out there and you can't see either bank. You just keep on going. It doesn't much matter why you're on the bridge in the first place."

I raised the window to let Bat in and fed him, probably for the third or fourth time today, but who was counting. Then I rinsed our cups. Deborah sat watching. Bat lifted his head from the bowl to assure himself that no one was likely to fly in under radar and get his food, then went back to eating. Deborah yawned.

"Where *I'm* going is to bed. You?"

"Maybe I'll try getting some work done."

"Don't stay up too late, love," she said, reclaiming her legs and letting them take her upstairs to bed.

When Deborah was gone, I took a bottle of Ja-maican ginger beer from the refrigerator and went out to the slave quarters. I wasn't writing books anymore, not for years, but habits hang around like ghosts or id-iot children that won't be got rid of, and sometimes late at night, still, I'd find myself sitting expectantly be-fore the computer. Instead of writing books, I reviewed them. Every few weeks Daniels (last name only, on the official name tag) rang the bell and pulled from her bag a bulky padded envelope bearing the logo of the *Times-Picayune, Washington Post, Boston Review.*

This one, a biography of Kenneth Fearing, had ar-rived a month or so back, so I must be close to dead-line on it. Fearing, who had achieved celebrity as a leftist poet and mystery novelist in the Thirties and Forties, was now almost wholly forgotten, yet another victim of what he himself had called the magic eraser of silence. Fiercely antiestablishment, a man to whom literary acclaim could mean only the containment of any truly challenging writing, Fearing would have found publication of *Floor of the Blue Night* by an academic press (according to his mood of the moment) amusing, ironic or abhorrent. I opened again onto the book's heavily indented pages, thickets of inset quotations and citations like broad stone stairs, like archways, and pulled out my notes, jotted on a typing sheet folded in half.

Then I put the book down, turned off the light and sat peering out. Bat had joined me, an indistinct, inert lump like a small gray haystack on the desk by the window. *A family,* I told Deborah, with no idea that, even as I said it, already my family had begun shrinking.

In preparation for writing the review I'd looked up a half-remembered poem assembled by Fearing's contemporary, Alfred Kreymborg, from headlines of the day.

> DOUBLE MURDER IN A HARLEM FLAT.
> CREW LOST WHEN LINER SINKS AT SEA.
> CHINAMAN BOILS RIVAL IN A VAT.
> COOLIDGE SURE OF MORE PROSPERITY.
> EARTHQUAKE SHAKES THE WHOLE
>   PACIFIC COAST.
> MORE FOLK OWN FORD CARS THAN
>   FOLK WHO CAN'T.
> KU KLUX KLAN WATCH ANOTHER
>   NEGRO ROAST. . . .

It was in the Thirties, Fearing's time, that America turned itself into an urban society. It was also, with the proliferation of mass media, when the great divide began developing between high and low art, and Fearing carried that divide within him, on the one hand consciously adopting a kind of writing that limited him, on the other finding within those limits a release of creative powers that otherwise might never have been available to him. Populists like James Agee, and in his own way Fearing, rejected belief that the old high art held some possibility of salvation. Now art, all art, had been democratized, leveled, marked down for quick sale. Now it could only be packaged and repackaged and packaged again to fill the unending need for consumer goods and the media's relentless demand for product: distilled into streams of sweet-tasting poison.

Little doubt that Agee, Fearing and the rest over-stated the case. But in their mixture of populist pride and sadness at the decline of a higher culture lay something vivid and luminous, the apprehension of one of those rare moments when society visibly, ut-terly changes, and the sense of loss that sweeps over us then. That stream of poison, too, is a thing we all recognize.

Blacks more than most.

The poison goes down from generation to genera-tion like the dissimulation and mimicry our forebears learned in order to survive, never saying what they really thought, putting their distress signals in code, till now, at this late hour in America's history and our own, we no longer know, maybe can't know, who we are or what we think.

Year by year by year the poison drips in. We're told it will heal us.

5

'D got up that morning (off the bench, so to speak), taken a long look at the reef of bottles, and climbed upstairs to bed. During the day I awoke several times and lay there listening to the old house's creaks and groans, remembering Whitman's *I think I will do nothing for a long time but listen/And accrue what I hear unto myself,* before falling back asleep. I got up for good when I heard Deborah down in the kitchen. It was dark.

"And here we thought you'd become just another brave explorer claimed by the desert," she said when I stumbled in.

"Bad news, I'm afraid. We had to kill the camels for food. And the bwana, of course."

"Bwana first, I hope."

"Damned right. Not much meat on Ol' Massuh, though. Tell me there's coffee."

"I was thinking about making some. You can chew the beans, if you're really desperate."

"Desperate, yes—but chewing beans would only remind me of the camels. I loved those camels."

"You *do* need coffee."

That was the first pot, as we sat idly talking, both of us too tired to give much thought to food or other routines of the day. We pulled various corners, edges and butt ends of cheese out of the fridge and ate them with the remains of a loaf of French bread. Deborah had stopped off at her set designer's apartment after leaving the flower shop, and it was now past nine. I'd slept, in bed as opposed to on bench, fourteen hours.

"I just didn't have the heart to wake you this morning when I came down. You were, by the way, doing a fine imitation of Bat, half on the bench and half off, no bones anywhere."

I squeezed both eyes shut and opened them again: Bat, wincing.

"You didn't get caught in the storm, then?" she asked.

"Only the beginnings of it. Which is just as well, from what I saw this morning. I'm surprised the streets were clear."

"They weren't. Passable, though. Everything bleached-out and blasted-looking, but with this brilliant sun and bright blue sky overhead. There had to have been all kinds of trash in the streets, tree limbs, trash cans, African drums, a bloated politician's body or two, but I guess the rain washed most of it away."

So, veering from prattle about Aristophanes and the play to news of her day at the shop, the latest on Pakistan's earthquake and the saga of my purposeless sit-in at Joe's, we went on talking till almost midnight, when Deborah cashed in the chip or two she had left and left the casino.

Coming back in from the slave quarters, I'd brought Fearing's spirit with me. Kenneth and I sat together in the dark not talking for a couple more hours. Bat followed me in, too, made another plea for food and, failing, curled up beside me on the chair's overstuffed, well-worn, moderately clawed arm.

I was sitting in pretty much the same place and attitude when Deborah came down the next morning. I'd had three or four hours' sleep upstairs myself, and now I was contemplating piles of laundry that needed doing. An Iwo Jima of whites, Allegheny of darks, a veritable Everest of colors. Where was Teddy Roosevelt when you needed him to go storming up these hills and take them? Even if the famous footage, and in large part the event itself, was faked.

"It's a start," Deborah said, "kind of. Which one's Krakatoa?"

"You're always complaining that I don't sort things properly."

"I just had in mind not putting everything in the washer at once, Lew. It somehow escaped me that the creation of new continents would be involved." She looked ceilingward, as though for steerage. "Oh well. Just passing through."

"City be full of tourists. Always underfoot. Speaking of which: any sign of David?"

"I didn't hear him this morning. Want me to go look?"

"He'd be up and about if he were here. I suspect he'll wander home when he's—as my father always said—of a mind to."

She went on to the kitchen, where I heard her rummaging: cabinet doors chattered, a drawer slid shut with the sound of an arrow thunking into its target. Dull smack of the refrigerator door opening. Minutes later she walked into the front hallway. A voice, none of which I could make out, unrolled on the answering machine. Then she was there in the doorway.

"Lew, you better come listen to this."

She wore a light green housecoat that matched the glass in her hand turning the orange juice within a sickly color.

"It's the third one," she said, pushing the button on the machine. "It must be from last night. Neither of us thought to check."

Mr. Griffin, this is Marie at Book News. I don't seem to have an e-mail address on file for you. We were wondering if you might have time to review a new translation of Cendrars for us. Give us a call? Thanks.

The second caller had so much trouble trying to say what he wanted that, after repeated stammering, he finally hung up.

Then the third. Jeanette's voice.

Lew, are you there? . . . I guess not . . . Can you call me when you get in? It's Don, Lew. He's been shot.

When the elevator doors opened on the second floor, three heads turned towards me. Two of the heads nodded. The owner of the largest of them came to meet me.

"Griffin," he said.

"Santos."

No hand was offered. Cops don't much like shaking hands. And when all was said and done, Santos himself, though his skin was as dark as my own, didn't much favor black men. No way in hell we were ever going to like one another, his attitude told me; but since I was a friend of Don's, he always treated me with deference. Don's retirement had left him chief of detectives.

"What happened?"

"Jeanette called you, right?"

I nodded.

"She told you Don's been shot."

"And that's the whole of what I know."

One of the other cops approached, and Santos stepped away for a moment to confer.

"We had kind of a send-off for Walsh last night," he said upon return. "Nothing formal, just a lot of us who wanted to get together and say hey, we're here, we appreciate what you've been doing all this time. Man did a fuckin' hero's job for a lotta years. You think anyone noticed? Anyone but us? So we got together at O'Brien's, a bar down on—"

"I know it."

"Yeah. Yeah, sure you do." His eyes met mine. O'Brien's was the closest thing New Orleans had to a cop's bar. Citizens knowing cop stuff is another thing cops don't much like. "Anyhow, Tony Colado snagged a cake half the size of a football field from his uncle's bakery, a deli a lot of the guys eat at up on Magazine kicked in a tray of sandwiches, like that. Whole thing ran maybe five in the afternoon to eight, eight-thirty."

Automatic doors from the ICU sprang open and a young man in blue scrubs ambled through. The scrubs, probably the largest available, struggled to cover the man's chest and bulky shoulders. Weightless blond hair clung to his scalp like damp flower petals; a tiny silver and blue-enamel cross hung from one ear. Beckoning for me to come along, Santos went to meet him.

"Dr. Lieber," he said. "This is Lew Griffin, he and the Captain go way back."

Don's rank and title had changed several times over the years. When he first took the job, not too long after we met, he'd been chief of detectives and a captain. Then sometime in the Seventies the department kicked him up to major. Twenty years later he'd become, at least briefly, maybe permanently—by this time I'd lost track, and he probably had too—an assistant superintendent. But cops don't take to change any better than they do to handshakes and citizens knowing things about them, and for most of the men he worked with, those to whom he wasn't just Walsh, he'd remained the Captain.

Dr. Lieber held out hands that looked like a steel-worker's and we shook.

"There's no real change, sir. Vital signs are stable, the bleeding's under control. He had developed, as I told you before, a secondary pneumothorax—free air in the chest, and hardly surprising in cases like this—but that's been taken care of. He's breathing on his own, without difficulty, though we're keeping him on the ventilator as a precaution."

"Is he conscious?"

"Not yet. Everything considered, we'd just as soon he'd stay under a while longer. The rabbit puts his head up, I'll—"

"Rabbit?"

"Sorry, it's been a long day. Just something we say all the time around here, among ourselves: that our job in ER is to pull rabbits out of hats and sometimes they don't even give us the hat. What I meant, first time there *is* a change, I'll let you know. Or if I'm not available, the resident on call will."

"Thank you."

"No need to. It's my job. I take the job seriously. So, apparently, did your friend in there."

Dr. Lieber turned and, pushing the doors open, went back into the ICU. The other cops immediately came over. Santos told them what had been said, then the two of us stepped away. We stood near the wall, in a narrow channel bounded by the ICU doors and an unmanned information desk, looking out. Beyond our dull oblong of an island, visitors and hospital personnel swarmed everywhere, pushing carts, carrying flowers and paper bags of belongings, rubbing at eyes or the backs of necks, embracing. The cover of brochures stacked on a table nearby read *Are you ready for Him?*

"Walsh stopped on the way home, at a Circle K just around the corner from his apartment. He went in, the guys were already there. He pulled some milk out of the cooler, started toward the register, then went back and got a six-pack. The store owner says he could see him staring into the glass door like he was trying to decide what kind of beer. Afterwards he figured that was why Walsh went after the beer in the first place—just so he could take a look around, without having it be obvious.

"There's two of them, one guy standing over by the magazines while the other one pretends he's playing this video game. Only there's no noise from the game machine, see, and it's like all of a sudden the one standing there by the machine, he's the one with the gun, thinks of this and starts getting nervous. Walsh and this guy start walking toward the register at the same time. The guy's reaching in under his jacket for the piece when Walsh says, Hey buddy, have a beer, and chunks the six-pack right at him. Guy jerks back, his feet slip and he goes down, but the piece goes off anyway. Then the six-pack hits him square in the face. That, the fall when he slams his head, and the store owner's jumping the counter and doing some slamming of his own with a baseball bat puts this mook down for the count. The other one's history by now. Long gone.

"But then the store owner, a Mr. Chadras, looks over and sees Walsh lying there with his service revolver drawn and blood streaming out all around him. He's having trouble breathing, too. But Mr. Chadras, it turns out, was a doctor back in his own country. He grabs a piece of gauze and some Vaseline off the shelf and slaps it over the hole in Walsh's chest. Saved his life, the paramedics say.

"Boy that did this looks all of nineteen. We tried running him, but the computer just started spitting out empties. Those weren't all that got spit out last night, either."

Santos took a small box from his pocket, the kind jewelry comes in.

"I ain't saying this was right, Griffin—or how it came about. Crew that booked him sent it up late last night. Boy had this tooth he was proud of. You know how they used to have those gold caps? Well, somehow or another this kid had one of those."

Santos lifted the box top. The gold tooth lay on a nest of cotton batting. Blood still adhered to the upper edge. A few strands of the cotton were stained pink.

Santos shrugged and put the box back in his pocket. "What can I say?"

For some reason, wildly, I thought of Don telling me he'd become a detective mainly because he could write a complete sentence, which put him miles ahead of the competition. I also remembered another time, years later, when I'd come upon him in a spectacularly sleazy bar deep in what was then no-man's-land below the Quarter. "Out of your element, aren't you?" I'd said. He sat for a moment peering into his glass. "Not really. I'm like you, Lew. I take my element with me."

Or another time, many years later, when my life had bottomed out. Some of his men had scraped me off the walls of a bar out on Jefferson Highway and taken me to Mercy. When I woke blank as a slate, no idea what had happened and more than a few days gone, Don was sitting beside me. Neither of us spoke for a while. Then he said, "What are you gonna do, Lew: there's nowhere to go but on."

"Appreciate your filling me in, Santos."

He nodded.

"You think I can see him?"

"Just family for now. Doctor says they'll let us in tomorrow, assuming everything goes right. I figure we go in, there's no problem with you coming along."

"Thanks."

"No problem."

"What about Jeanette? She with him?"

"Sent her home to get some rest. Took some talking and fast footwork on my part."

"I expect it did. Guess I should go by, then, see what I can do."

"Yeah, she'd like that."

I stepped off our island and started for the door.

"Hey, Griffin, you need a ride?" Santos called. I turned back to decline, but saying, "Sure you do," Santos called out again: "Whitaker, you wanna give Griffin here a ride over to Captain Walsh's?"

The cop I didn't know detached himself. We went down and out and across the alley to where his gray Crown Victoria was parked by a Dumpster. ("You wouldn't believe what shows up in there," he said.) Moments later we pulled into traffic. Whitaker's radio had come on, turned low, when he hit the key, one of those stations that alternates its own trademark brand of news with talk shows about welfare abuse, the conspiracy of world government and the dangers of water fluoridation. Whitaker took two sticks of gum from a package the size of a paperback *War and Peace* jammed into where the ashtray had once been. He was, I figured, around thirty.

Much of the drive uptown became a kind of down-and-out Grey Line tour.

"That's the Billies," Whitaker said as we passed the slablike, mostly roofless shell of a building. Two men inside sat on boxes at a battered old spool cable, having breakfast from the look of it. I half expected them to lift their cups to us in greeting. "Billy Williams and Billy Nabors. Been there over a year now. Came down from Minnesota, Nebraska, one of them places. Say they just couldn't take the cold no more."

Some blocks further on we passed a sixtyish woman wearing a red wool sweater, pink ballet tutu with baggy, lime-green tights, and purple-and-orange sneakers.

"Squeezebox Sally. Makes the rounds on Maple Street every night, all those restaurants and bars up there, with her accordion. Comes up to a table and asks people, usually couples, what they want to hear, but it all sounds the same, mainly just her pushing and pulling at the box, hitting keys at random. Word is, she used to be some kind of piano virtuoso. Word is also that now she's deaf as a board. Her big finish is always the same: she turns around, bends over and tosses up her skirt."

"I guess there are some things in New Orleans's rich cultural life that I'd just as soon miss out on," I said.

"Could definitely put you off your lasagna."

We were almost to Don's by this time. Whitaker took a right by the Circle K where Don had been shot.

"Bonner"—the other cop, that I knew, from back at the hospital—"says you write books."

"I used to. Used to do a lot of things."

"Didn't we all," Whitaker said, pulling up at the curb.

6

EGULARS knew him as Dog Boy. He could be found each morning and late afternoon, accompanied by the elderly black man who looked after him, in the small park a block and a half away, riverside, from our house. Whenever someone brought a dog into the park, the boy would drop to all fours and stare into the animal's eyes. Most of them stared back, boy and dog transfixed before one another, fused in the press of their concentration to something like a single entity; I had seen lap dogs, poodles and Dobermans the size of small cars standing there by him, turning their heads that curious way dogs have, keening in puzzled kinship. Dogs were chiefly what people brought to the park, hence the name, but the boy's sympathies extended well beyond. Once I observed him by the ironwork fence, back bent to an S curve, chattering away with the squirrel atop it. Another time, what must have been an escaped domestic parrot came to rest, bobbing, in an azalea, while boy and bird, faces but inches apart, rolled, swiveled and ducked heads in tandem.

Lester Johnson had worked for the boy's family, as a shoe repairman in a store they owned, for over forty-two years, long after people gave up on having shoes repaired; long, too, after Lester's arthritic hands had grown unable to hold the necessary tacks, narrow-headed hammers, awls and needles, and his eyes un-suited to such detail work. His wife, Emmie, had cared for the boy at first, just as she'd brought up the family's older children, all of them even then off to college or making their way in the world, but when the boy was three and the family first coming to the realization that something was not quite right, Emmie had died. Her blood pressure shot up not to be brought down, circulation faltered and began to fail, every treatment seemed to further complicate things, and one quiet Saturday afternoon as Lester stood by the bed he watched her, with a single long breath, let go. Four days later he shut up the shoe store for the last time and took over Emmie's duties.

Over the course of the first couple of years we saw one another in the park, Lester and I had begun speaking. Over the next two or three we'd gradually progressed to brief exchanges. Only this past year, and without its ever emerging as a conscious decision for either of us, I think, had we taken to sitting together and talking.

Lester was never less than properly, one might say elegantly, dressed, shoes buffed to a high shine, coat and tie even on the steamiest of New Orleans days. If sometimes the clothes were a bit worn, well, so were the two of us. And if coat and slacks didn't quite go to-gether, what matter: we were both used to mis-matches in our lives. Today he wore a drip-dry white shirt with long, pointed collar, tan tie with Hawaiian beach scene, mustard-colored coat, maroon slacks hitched up to show brown nylon socks with figures of dogs as clockwork. The continent of Lester ended at two-tone shoes, off-white on tan.

He looked up as I approached and, though no one else sat on the bench with him, moved the boy's backpack closer to himself to make room. A bottle of chocolate drink peeked from out his twisted fingers.

"Lewis. A pleasure as always. Must of been, what, Thursday a week ago, I saw you last?"

"Thereabout." Right now I had about as much time sense as Doo-Wop.

"Thursday," Lester said, nodding to confirm it.

We didn't shake. I'd done so once, noting in his face (though he was too polite ever to have told me this) the pain it brought him. What I saw in his face now was something different, something I never stopped marveling at. Lester had a genius for attentiveness, for making whatever you said to him, whatever you *might* say to him, seem vitally important. Everything about him signaled that he'd never before heard the like of it, and that he valued your choosing him to share it with as much as he valued the information itself.

"You've been busy, then."

I told him about Don, that I'd just come from seeing Jeanette. She had insisted on making coffee for us, listening for the gurgle as we sat waiting in the front room and, once that had come and subsided, finding only hot water in the carafe, having forgotten to put in coffee. The can of French Market still sat there on the counter by the sink.

"Tough on her," Lester said.

I nodded.

"She just have to be tougher. Your friend's okay, though?"

"Going to be, anyway. How're things with you?"

"Things moving right along, Lewis. Like they do

most days, 'f we just think to take notice of them. Billy Boy over there seems to have him a new woman. Thinks he might, anyways." I followed Lester's nod to a large tan-and-white pigeon strutting before another, smaller bird, periodically bowing and bobbing. "Gertie came up missing some weeks back. Been together a long time. They mate for life, you know. But if one of them dies, sometimes the other one will take a new mate. And it looks like Billy Boy's of a mind to do just that."

When Billy Boy turned to make another pass, I saw that the bird's foot was clubbed, digits curled back under and withered into a ball, burrlike. Some portion of what I'd assumed to be courtship posturing in fact derived from a rolling limp as he stepped onto the damaged foot.

"City's hard on them," Lester said.

"Hard on us all."

"*That's* God's truth."

Cooing at him and ducking her head twice, Billy's new lady strolled to the pond for an aperitif, a delicate beakful of scummy water. Billy joined her. There were so many insects skittering across the pond's surface that they looked like cabs at rush hour in midtown Manhattan.

Lester's gold signet ring jangled against the bottle as he raised his hand to gesture, long index finger unfurling from the rest. It spent some time unfurling. Its nail was the size of a demitasse spoon, almost perfectly flat. "Not many birds do that, drink directly by immersing their bills and sucking. Pigeons are one of the few." Every week, Lester had told me, he carted home an armful of books from the public library. Whenever he became interested in a subject, pigeons for instance, or ancient Greece, he read everything the library had. "During Egyptian times—"

Lester stopped because the boy had come up to

us. He stood there making whimpering sounds, eyes puffy and red though no tears fell. He held out his hands together, palms up. In them a pigeon's head lolled as it tried to focus, to understand where it found itself, to get a fix on this latest in a procession of dangers, the exact nature of the catastrophe. Even as we watched, the head fell. Its eyes filmed over as light left them.

"It's gone, child," Lester said. "Dead, like the others."

Lester and the boy went off behind a stand of oleander where, with a stick and a fragment of sharp-edged wood, they dug a shallow grave for the bird. I offered to help, but Lester declined, saying it would be better if they did it themselves. So I sat watching, warmed as always by the relationship these two had, each in his own way forever the outsider, one of them having seen, suffered and survived most of what the world had for him, one given eternal youth and thus forever given to seeing the world anew. That was good, to a point. But the pain came as strongly each time as did the wonder; it never diminished.

"Others?" I asked when Lester rejoined me. The boy, whom he had left sitting by the grave, now walked to the edge of the park and stood pressed against the mesh fence there, motionless, like a statue caught in netting.

"Close to a dozen this past week, I expect. Someone poisoning them, is what they say. Almost have to be."

"And no one's looking into it?"

"Lewis. They don't care 'bout all our young colored men dying out there for no good reason, who in this town you think's gonna bother themselves over a few pigeons more or less?"

"You do."

Lester smiled. "Yes sir, I expect I do," he said after a moment. "So does my boy over there. And that, I expect, is the *long* list."

"Maybe not."

Lester stood to carry the squat bottle over to the garbage, dropped it in. Another man materialized at his side and pulled it out. This one carried two black plastic bags bulked and lumpy with objects and wore a gray pinstripe suit over a soiled white shirt with tail out, dress shoes with tassels. Tassel fringes poked out every which way. The outside edges of the heels were worn down to slivers. When Lester came back to the bench, the newcomer followed, sitting between us, by the boy's pack.

"You come here all the time, don't you?" he said. "I know, I see you. Started me thinking what I had that you'd like." He spent the next half-hour pulling various items from his bags and offering them to Lester, a plastic clock with one hand, a pair of white earth shoes gone fish-belly gray, a sandwich bag of paper clips, rubber bands and gum erasers, whether with a thought to profit or as gifts never becoming clear; I'm not sure he knew. Lester would tell him he wasn't interested and the man would talk for a few more minutes about people in the neighborhood, where he'd obviously spent his entire life, about this one who had been arrested or was in the hospital or that one who had suddenly attacked family members with a crowbar or electric carving knife, before starting up again with "I've got just the thing for you" and dipping back into his bags.

"Can't use it, sorry," Lester said for the twentieth or thirtieth time.

"I understand, I understand." He sat quietly for a moment looking off towards the line of palm trees across the street, then towards the fence where the boy still stood immobile. Messages might come through at any time, from any source, any direction. "That's your boy, right?"

Lester nodded.

"Fine young man. I know, I watch him here, I can see that. They *are* a pleasure, aren't they?" He was shoulder-deep in his bags again. "Look, you don't mind," he said, "I've got just the thing for the boy here. He'll love it," coming up with a green rubber scuba mask. The seals were rusted, the straps rotten. "Perfect fit."

7

Back in basic, over near Mobile, they put me in a barracks full of white men not altogether reconciled to their new living arrangements. Working beside us was one thing. These weren't, after all, your educated, privileged young white gentlemen— most of those one way or another got out of serving— so it's not like they weren't used to working on farms or in factories or loading trucks alongside Negroes. They'd even got used to using the same bathrooms. But this, sleeping beside us, eating every meal with us, this was something else again.

I'd lie in bed at night after lights-out watching the play of shadows from palm trees on the wall and listening to the wind. It seemed to me that summer that the wind was coming in off the beach always, rushing breathless towards us from somewhere else, washing up in great waves like the tides themselves.

A few days before my own wave peaked, I had watched them grab one of the other blacks, a slow, slightly backward, ever-friendly boy from Texas, out behind the latrine. He'd been lipping off to them, they said—and beat him badly. I had seen it happening, then gone on by, and hadn't stepped up to them on it. I was still worrying over that, trying to find a place inside myself I could put it. But if I did step up to them, I kept telling myself, they'd only come for me next. At that point I hadn't learned that it didn't matter, they'd most likely come for me anyway.

They did, maybe two weeks later, about two in the morning. I heard the springs on one of their beds, then the other, and could follow their progress towards me by the creaking of floorboards. I lay unmoving, one arm hanging off the side of my bunk. Outside, a sudden gust of wind caught in the trees and bounced like a thrown ball from branch to branch.

Moments before they reached me, I jumped to my feet. The radio my mother had just sent me came along; I swung it on its cord in two quick circles above my head before crashing it against that of the nearest of my attackers. I heard the crunch of something internal, radio, head, giving way. The man went down and didn't move.

Turning to the other, I pulled out the antenna I'd taken off the radio earlier and with a flick of my wrist extended it. I went at him with it as though it were whip and foil in one, slashing, slashing again. Deep cuts opened on the hands he held up to try and protect himself, on his face, on neck and arms. When he began backing away, I went with him, never letting up, slashing, tearing. He tripped, tripped again and this time couldn't catch himself, falling backwards against the wall.

Thanks, Mom.

During all this, no one else in the barracks had moved or spoken. Now a voice from the far end said: "Those boys through?"

"They be done with, all right," another said.

Then the first again: "You okay, Griffin?"

I said I was.

"That's good."

A pause. I could hear my heart thudding.

"Right shame those boys had to tear into each other that way. Who's have thought there was bad blood between them? Always looked to be close. Just goes to show. . . . Guess we'd best get the sergeant in here, tell him what happened. Reckon they'll be in stir awhile."

8

A FEW days later, I was able to tell Don: "You look like shit."

I don't know why I had been thinking about that incident back in basic on my way to see Don. Just musing on mayhem in general, maybe. Or sending telegrams to myself in code. Sometimes memories are like dreams, artifacts of unknowable civilizations falling into ruin even as you approach them.

Santos had come in with me, then after a few minutes' badinage left us alone. Don was in one of fifteen glassed-in rooms set like petals of a flower around a central nurses' station. Phones rang unrelentingly at the station, buzzers and mysterious, unsettling pneumatic sounds came from other rooms, snatches of conversation ricocheted off walls and ceiling.

"Well, that's some comfort, at least. Good to know I look better than I feel."

"You'll want this coffee." I set the cup down by him. "And today's newspaper."

"You could have saved yourself the trouble—"

"—and brought last week's, I know." It was an old joke with us: they're all the same. "Doctors tell me you're going to live."

"Ah, still more reassurance. Interesting . . . They look to be happy with this news?"

"Hard to say. Consensus seems to be you're one thoroughgoing, uncooperative son of a bitch."

"All because I told that male nurse I couldn't use a bedpan, never had been able to use a bedpan, and if he brought the damn thing in here one more time I'd put it away for good where no one would ever find it. You could tell he was giving it some thought."

"On the other hand, they probably figure that means they'll eventually get rid of you."

Don sipped tepid coffee. "My God, that's wonderful. You forget all the small things, don't you? Take them for granted. Taste of coffee, or the feel of clean sheets against your skin. When maybe in the end they're what's important, what stays with you once most of the rest is gone."

I sat by his bed. "You're going to be okay."

"We always are, you and me."

"Way a philosopher friend of mine once put it, we carry our okay with us."

He laughed. A tube went from the upper part of his left chest to a plastic box sitting on the floor beside his bed. When he laughed, valves of some sort fluttered in the box, making a sound like grasshopper wings. Don looked down at the box. Then he laughed again, at a different tempo and rhythm. "Hey, maybe I could learn a few tunes while I'm lying here." He shifted on the bed. Plastic mattress covers crinkled. "Feel like something from a horror movie, all these tubes growing out of me."

"Ze pain, it ees not-ing. Endure it, Herr Valsh-

man, endure it in ze knowledge that zoon jew vill be
. . . more than human."

Don finished his coffee and set the cup down with
a soft click.

"I'm tired, Lew. Used up."

"Been a rough few days. Then there's that retirement thing, wear down the best of men."

"You see a wheelchair coming in?"

"Yeah, there's one right outside your room."

"You wanta get it? I don't think I can walk and
carry all this shit. Hell, I'm not sure I can walk at all."

"We're going somewhere?"

"Just down the hall."

Seeing me fetch the chair, a nurse came flying out
of the central station and through the room's open
doorway with a shrill litany of can't-allow-its and ab-
solutely-nots. *Rose Price-Jamison*, her name tag read. I
stood quietly by and let her and Don talk it through,
their discourse a stew of pigheadedness, tacit invective
and (for me) the all-too-familiar condescension of
medical personnel. Authorities were called to bear, a
charge nurse, a baffled and battle-fatigued surgical resident, a hospital administrator; finally Dr. Lieber, who
after listening to the resident's summary said more or
less, Man thinks he can do it, let him. Miss Price-Jamison helped us gather up tubes, monitor lines and IVs
and hang them strategically about the chair.

"And you wonder why phrases like 'thoroughgoing, uncooperative son of a bitch' follow you around."

"Image is everything."

"Yeah. Well right now you look like something
from a cheapie version of *Mad Max*. Big finale's gonna
be you and the bad guy chasing one another in wheelchairs across the wasteland." I rolled us out into the
circle. It suddenly occurred to me how much the lay-
out of the ICU resembled a roulette wheel. "Where
we going?"

"Prison ward. Up one floor, go to the end of the corridor, Santos says."

We shared the elevator with another reverse-rickshaw pair, pusher and pushee alike twentyish black men. Urine in the bag attached to the latter's wheelchair was the dull red of rust. His head kept falling onto his chest, then he'd catch himself and come around again. His unfocused eyes were that startling gold color you see often around New Orleans.

I pushed Don off the elevator and down the hall. He thumbed the buzzer by locked double doors beyond which only a wall could be seen. Within moments a voice issued from the tiny speaker: "Can I help you?"

"Yes, ma'am. This is Captain Don Walsh, NOPD. There's an officer on duty in there, I take it?"

"Yes, sir."

"Could you ask him to step out here, please?"

"I would, sir, but he can't—"

"Just to the door."

"Yes, sir."

"Thanks."

Shortly an officer stepped into sight around the wall and stood close behind the doors, squinting out. Not old, in his forties maybe, but had an old man's gait and posture. His neck jutted forward rather than upward from his neck, making him look turtlelike. He moved head and neck together from left to right and back, then smiled with a lipless mouth.

"What can I do for you, Captain?"

"Boy apprehended during a robbery over on Louisiana, a Circle K—he doing okay?"

"I think. Looks like someone took a tenderizer to him. Bad concussion, they say. But I've seen 'em hurt far worse get up and do more damage."

"I want to see him."

For just a moment the officer looked doubtful, as

though he were going to recite regulations Don probably knew better than anybody else in the department, but then he said "You got it," and sprang the door. He hesitated again before asking, "Be okay if I came along?"

"You bet."

"Down this way."

"What do we know about him?" Don asked.

"About this much." The officer held up thumb and index finger joined in a circle. "Looks to be about eighteen, says he's sixteen. No ID on him, no police, juvenile or court records. No mailing address or record of residence. Not a shred of paperwork anywhere, that we've been able to find."

"Boy doesn't exist."

"Probably more of them like that out there than you'd think."

"Could be."

"Joe Papi works that ward pretty hard," the officer continued after a moment. "Came up there himself. He says he remembers seeing the kid around, starting maybe four, five months back."

"Boy was on the streets."

The officer nodded. With his weird neck, it put me in mind of those dogs with bobbing heads you see in cars, on back window ledges.

We were at the door by then. Inside, looking a bit like Claude Rains, the kid had the bed cranked up high and was sitting there watching Ricki Lake. One after another, fat black women hanging four-fifths out of various outfits strutted from the wings, paraded through the audience and settled into overstuffed chairs onstage before launching into harangues about how sexy they were and how they could have any man they wanted anytime. *Big and Bootieful* showed at one corner of the screen, the first *B* stylized to suggest breasts, the second tipped on its side and bulging ludicrously in a caricature of buttocks. Wholly untouched by irony or by any sensibility at all, this spectacle was a kind of assault, as insulting to the audience as it was degrading to the women. Still, it bore manifest of a certain crude innocence; and to every appearance the kid found it hilarious.

He looked over finally at the three of us crowding into the room, eyes in their field of bandage moving from Don and his barge to me, the toter.

"Ain't that *always* the way it is, though."

Then his eyes went back to Don. Briefly his tongue, shockingly pink, naked-looking, larval, protruded past bandages.

"You don't look so good neither, man."

Don glanced over his shoulder at me. I shrugged. "Second opinion."

"Shit, man." The kid shook his head. "Shit." His eyes went back to the TV. "Look-a that. Man could hide under there, no one goan ever find him. Whoa! Hold that thing still, mama!"

He watched several moments before saying, "I'd lack that beer now, officer."

Don smiled up at him. "Could use one myself. More than one."

"I hear that." His eyes swung towards me. "You think they pay them bitches or what, they go up there, shake it loose like that? Why they do that?"

"Got me. Maybe they just want the attention."

"*Got*ta be it."

"My name's Don Walsh. How you doing?"

"Man, whatchu care? You the one did this. Now you goan come in here, 'pologize?"

Don didn't say anything more, just kept eye contact, his expression neutral. After a moment the kid said, "I'm okay, man. You know." Then he looked away.

"Yeah. Well, case you didn't notice, I ain't gonna be up dancing much sooner than you are."

"Won't look near as good when you *do*, neither."

"That's for damn sure. . . . You ever get tired of watching that TV?"

"Sometimes. Mornings 'specially. Ain't never much on then. News 'n' shit, all them ol' dudes in their richass suits."

"Could I get you some books or something?"

"What the fuck'm I gonna do with books?"

"Okay. . . . How about this, then? We're both gonna be here awhile. You don't mind, I could come over now and then, maybe a couple times a day, we could hang out."

"Why would you wanta do that?"

"Hey, there's not any more to do in my room than there is in yours. Nothing else, it'd help pass the time. We could talk." Don glanced up at the TV. "Or just watch all these fine women."

"You wanta come, how'm I gonna stop you? Yeah. Yeah, I guess that be all right."

"Good."

Don motioned, and I started backing out the door. Just as I was about to swing the chair around, the kid said, "My name's Derick. Derick Soames. Most ever'one calls me Jeeter, though."

"Good to meet you, Jeeter," Don said. "This is Lew. You're on the streets, he's a good man to know."

"He is, huh, him and his richass suit. Why? He goan save me from getting myself punked by the like of you?" What might have been a laugh almost made it out of him.

We started out the door again.

"Don Walsh."

"Yeah?"

"I did used to play some checkers, back when I was a kid."

Don nodded.

"One more thing . . ."

"Okay."

"You know where my tooth is?"

9

THINGS are the mind's mute looking glass, Walter de la Mare, another on the long list of forgotten writers, said. And Whitman, that things, objects, are a coherent world to themselves, the "dumb, beautiful ministers of reality."

Certainly they become that when you're drunk. You watch for hours as shadows from a palm or banana tree toss heads, sway and sweep wings across the wall beside your bed, doing all the creative things you should be doing. Towels tossed on the floor by the tub suddenly seem to harbor both great beauty and codes never before suspected, kennings just beyond reach, the towels' folds and convolutions catching up, as a phonograph record does sound, those of your own mind.

Drinking also maroons you without provisions on the island of self. Like most other promises it makes, alcohol's vow of kinship, that it will bridge your life to others, smooth the way, proves false. Fooled again:

you're alone. The path remains treacherous—stones in your passway, as Robert Johnson would say. And not another footprint on the whole island.

Emerson: Wherever we go, whatever we do, self is the sole object we study and learn. A solipsism that America took to its clanky, pragmatic heart not as philosophy but as operator's manual. Humanism was from the first, of course, a matchless arrogance. And American individualism was humanism writ large, not just arrogant but colossally arrogant: Emerson's "infinitude of the private man" turned out for the masses like bins of polyester shirts marked down for quick sale, durable, practical, all but indestructible, unlovely.

Still and well enough, there on your island of Scotch or gin, palm trees swaying, mind become this curious suspension bridge built from scraps of driftwood and salvage, everything remains fraught with meaning. Whitman also wrote

> To me the converging objects of the universe
>   perpetually flow,
> All are written to me, and I must get what
>   the writing means

and I have to wonder if that's not what my life, all our lives, finally, are about, that imperative and the misreadings to which it forces us.

When I was a kid, parents would tell us not to cross our eyes because they'd get stuck and we'd never be able to uncross them, we'd have to walk around like that the rest of our lives. That's what introspection can come down to. You keep on with it, sinking through level after level, after a while you can't get back to the top. You just go on pounding out the same thoughts on the stone over and over, fitting your feet into old footprints. Alcohol's the same way.

Years ago, I'd known I was in trouble when I

found myself weeping uncontrollably over commercials on TV. A beleaguered housewife would smile around at her clean-as-new house, a couple's bitter arguments trickle away as they drove their car towards snow-capped mountains, a man meet his wife for dinner, horribly late, carrying flowers—and I'd sit there sobbing, shaking, ruined. I was supposed to connect with the world, not collide with it, I remember thinking. Back then I'd got on to the habit of reading, listening to music and watching TV all at the same time as I drank. I never failed to think of David Bowie as the alien sitting before his bank of TV screens all tuned to different programs in *The Man Who Fell to Earth*. But I'd discovered that, when I did this, something curious took place. That I was able to follow the TV show without difficulty wasn't surprising. But I found, and this *was* surprising, that I was more intimately connected with the music than at any other time, that it became impressed upon me in ways and to a degree it otherwise would not have been. And whatever books I read or half-read those times, whether Turgenev's *Fathers and Sons*, Vin Packer's *The Twisted Ones* or Himes's *The End of a Primitive*, remained with me forever.

Then one night it all turned to shit. I'd been listening to Mahler's Ninth, reading a novel set in Washington by some guy with a Greek name, and watching a movie in which a thirty-year-old actor playing the part of a high-school student confronted his girlfriend at a drive-in. She'd died in a car crash in the first twenty minutes of the film while riding with another young man but refused to stay put, clawing her way up out of the grave to come and tell the thirty-year-old that she'll love him forever, there by his locker at school when he swings the door shut, now showing up at the drive-in while he's on a date and rapping at his car window. "Forever," she tells him, rotted flesh and a few teeth falling away as she mouths the word. "How fuckin' long can forever be to a thirty-year-old!" I remember yelling at the screen. I'd been drinking pretty hard, apparently, harder than I thought or kept track of. I surfaced half a week or so later in the hospital, not Baptist or Touro or Mercy that time, but the state hospital over in Mandeville, this hulking, gray, utterly silent beast set among green trees and lawn where time was dipped in half-spoonfuls from the heart of glaciers and fossils deep in the earth. I was still going on about the movie as though it were real, as though everything in it had actually taken place.

The incidence of mental illness among Negroes is significantly higher than among the population at large, someone was telling me. This seemed to come from far away and from inside my head at the same time. I swam up, towards light. Away from the voice. Closer to the voice.

We sat facing one another across the kind of table you find in church basements and high school lunchrooms. It looked as if it had just been unpacked from its carton.

He looked the same way. Boy Doctor Ferguson, I thought, taking his name from the narrow slab of brass name tag above a pocket crammed with pens, rulers, tongue depressors, hemostats and, for all I knew, a dental drill. Ever alert to use of language when alert at all, I particularly admired that "population at large." B. D. Ferguson had sparse hair the color of cotton candy and as insubstantial. He kept reaching up to brush it down, pretty much a losing proposition, since our own breaths bouncing back from the walls would be enough to dislodge it again. Whether from allergies, chronic lack of sleep or tears shed for patients, Ferguson's eyes were shrimp-red. So, for quite different reasons, were mine. Men always have more in common than they think.

I had no idea, I said.

Few do. Why should you? Professionals who spend a lifetime studying it understand little enough. There's no doubt the gauges we use are biased. We've known that for years. Culturally biased, as with IQ tests. Add in poor prenatal care if any at all, poverty, discrimination, lack of access to medical services—

Think I read about that in *Partisan Review*. This to a man upon whom irony was wasted.

—it's a hopeless stew. Historically diagnosticians like myself —

Diagnosticians. Nice. And the dinosaur track of a metaphor there in the limestone. Hope for the boy after all?

—are far less reluctant, when confronted with minorities and those from lower socioeconomic levels, to attach such a potentially devastating diagnosis.

Well, I didn't tell him, that was not my experience of the thing, not at all. Nor did I patiently or otherwise explain that, being well outside our culture, he might have no idea how to read the codes our signals came wrapped in. That mistakenly he took our distrust at being delivered into his hands for paranoia, our dissembling as some innate inability to discern falsehood from truth, when in fact it's a highly developed form of just such discretion.

I've read the history your friend Don Walsh supplied the intake physician, B. D. went on. He's been quite helpful.

Afternoon sunlight stretched long fingers across the table. A phone rang in the next room. Two teenage boys with shaved heads walked past the window eating Eskimo Pies. Life goes on.

Your mother shows clear signs of schizophrenia. Has no friends to speak of, avoids family contact— perhaps there's been a rift of some sort? She lives alone, appears to have neither hobby nor outside interests nor, to all appearances, much of anything at all she enjoys or enjoys doing. I gather she leads a rigorously controlled life, every day exactly the same from hour to hour, growing upset at the slightest disturbance in her routine.

I sat watching this privileged young man, keeping track of sunlight popping knuckles on the tabletop and wondering how long after our talk before B. D. noted *inappropriate affect* in my chart. His handwriting would be cramped, precise. I'd flashed back to another interview, years before, with a psychiatrist who sat rocking in his desk chair the whole time, staring at me out of tiny round eyes with folds of fat like bite-size omelettes at the corner, neither of us speaking. I learned from the best.

The incidence of schizophrenia in the general population is approximately one in a hundred. As with so much else, we don't understand why, but among children of schizophrenics, the incidence jumps to one in ten.

Sometimes too, he went on when I remained silent, it skips a generation.

Jumps. Skips. There was a poem there somewhere. A limerick or jingle. At very least a groaningly bad joke.

Your son has a frank history of mood disorders, reclusiveness, abrupt life changes. All this giving way to intermittent periods of productive, purposeful behavior. Maybe you could tell me a little more about that.

After a while he said: Or maybe not.

After which (though his eyes continued to rise like twin red moons in my sky) my unsprightly self and B. D. Ferguson (certainly no son of the Fergus I knew from Joyce, O'Brien and the like) didn't have much to say to one another. We went on not saying it for six sessions in as many days.

Little chance that my girlfriend would love me forever, of course. With the taste of boiled meat, rice, iceberg lettuce and salty, limp vegetables in mouth and memory, slowly I came to realize this. She wasn't about to come back from the grave, reemerge from history's undiscovered country, float to the top of the lake, swim to shore and shamble, slaking away the whole time, towards wherever it was I'd gone on with my life. None of it had been a dream as, coming to, I'd first believed. Only another of society's makeshift facsimiles of dream, rags and tatters of movies, media, popular literature, this new mythology, that my homeless soul had taken for its own and worn into the street. Precious little protection. And how much shame could a man bear?

At the time I'm writing of, though, time of the storm and Alouette's second baby rather than that of hospital walkways like cloisters and young men of power with piggish red eyes (I've just read back through the past dozen or so pages to see where we've got to in all this), Deborah and I remained in sight of one another though borne steadily apart, Don and Jeanette were content on their island, David soon would return from scouting out copses and caves. New lives for us all rattled doors in frames. And I, freshly become a museum diorama, New Age man in his natural habitat, hunched not over campfires but before computers, sat inert in a circle of light at 3 A.M.

I had decided again, after an evening with Deborah, to get some work done. Write the Fearing review at least, since it was due or well past. Maybe start something else, who knows. Even pursue the notion for a novel I'd had a few weeks back in which the narrator would present himself to each of the other characters as a wholly different person. See which way, how far and how fast, that notion ran when chased full throttle. As always, the very idea of such work ne-

cessitated my removing to the slave quarters and sitting there staring out through windows so darkened
with dust and grime that you could safely watch
eclipses through them. Consisted, eventually, of turning on the computer. Its small dynamo whirred and
began a rapidly accelerating dialog with itself as Bat
minnowed through the half-open doorway to join me,
lugging in his wake a contingent of winged insects.
With age he'd become a semi-mobile solar battery. Besides food, only sunlight drew him, his days a pro-
gression from food bowl to sunshine spot and back.
Sunlight was far and away best, but if that proved un-
available, if he had to, he'd make do with artificial
sources. One favorite spot was at the back of my desk
about three inches below the desk lamp. Hoisting him
up there, most of the insects he'd brought in coming
along, I keyed in Microsoft Word and began reading
my notes for the novel. Halfway down the second
page, the ground gave way.

> I have no idea when you might find this—
> tonight, tomorrow, next week. I don't even
> know, really, how to begin it. Dad? Lew? I've
> never known what to call you. Are we friends?
> peers? father and son? A bit of all those, I sup-
> pose. And a bit of none.
>
> I remember something you told me Dylan
> Thomas said, That he'd lived with it a long time
> and knew it horribly well and couldn't explain
> it—whatever it was that drove him, beached him,
> bedeviled him. Much as I'd like to lay claim to
> something of that nature, my own situation, I'm
> afraid, is far less dramatic, far simpler: this sim-
> ple, desperate need to be alone that comes up
> within and overtakes me. Whatever the reason, I
> seem to be unable to remain myself when around
> others for too long a time. I lose focus, take on
> those others' properties and character, *their* pres-
> ence, *their* values and ambitions, while my own,

fought for so hard—not only the exercise of them, but the very recognition of them—begin to fade away.

I do love you, Lew. Dad. And these four years (four years!) have been amazing. I never thought I'd ever know anything like this. And I guess I must understand what families are about, now, for the first (I won't say the last) time. But I have to leave—as, once you've found this, I'll have done. You'll be sad, and will want to understand. We always have to understand, don't we, the two of us? (That's another thing I must get away from.) At some point Don Quixote, Alonso Quixano the Good, must die, and Cide Hamete Benengeli hang up his pen. Together and apart, they both had a good run. But it's time.

So it was that morning in its yellow hat came calling.

Six or a little after, Deborah emerged in housecoat and slippers and found me sitting on the porch. The Penguin Classics edition of Cervantes' masterpiece was open to page 240. A bottle of Scotch lay sideways on the warped floor.

"Lew?" she said.

And the dam of my eyes broke, and tears flooded the land.

10

As often transpires with organizations of a thoroughgoing liberal bent, it was difficult to find anyone at the community center who'd admit to being in charge. Simple caution, or some weird excess of democratic spirit? Winnowing my way from desk to desk, eventually I fetched up before that of a lady named Valerie LeBlanc, face so white it made the pale pink sweater she wore look like a burst of violent color, and stood there thinking both about her name and the fact that she'd claim responsibility. Cast of faces around us running, as they did, from coffee to jet.

"Yes, ma'am, if that's okay with you," I said in answer to her nonquestion. *And Alouette asked you to come by and pick up some work she could do at home.* "Didn't want to go rooting around her desk without saying something first." If mankind cannot bear too much reality, neither does it need too much truth told it. Use in moderation. Apply to a small, inconspicuous area first to test its effect. "That is, assuming I could even find it in here."

"So you're Lewis?" she said. "I don't believe we've seen you here before."

"Well, from the look of things, you could have a couple of extended families living in here full-time and never know it."

Long ago the place had begun life as a wine and liquor warehouse. Then for years it lay dormant until, during a brief period of progressive government (this oversight soon enough corrected), cascades of funds for "community improvement" became available. Delta Bottled Goods was reborn as Riverside Community Center and ever since, for some fourteen or fifteen years, it had been hanging out over the precipice with ropes afray, held aloft on half a broken wing, stupendous individual effort, all manner and forms of prayer. Now its cavernous spaces and bare, stained cement floor were strewn with desks and tables, some of them cobbled together from odd combinations of doors, squat filing cabinets or sawhorses, cinder blocks, planks, plastic milk crates, and studded with makeshift partitions formed of taller file cabinets, plywood and pegboard slabs lashed or nailed to the backs of desks, hastily constructed, slew-footed bulletin boards. The whole place still had much of the factory air about it and always would. Here, daily, dreams were refurbished, pills and loose threads cut from America's shabby egalitarian overcoat before it was passed along to new wearers.

Valerie LeBlanc removed her glasses: prolapsed teardrops, shell-gray, ruby rivets at apices. They swung on a gray cord about her neck, bare eyes springing forth with an unsuspected warmth, out of focus, vulnerable, immensely attractive.

"Alouette's fine, though," she said. Another non-question. Had she checked, or did she simply assume, with the mulish optimism of uncompromising well-wishers, that all in her vicinity must go smoothly?

"She is."

"And the child. A girl."

"LaVerne—after her mother."

She nodded. "LaVerne and I worked together at a women's shelter downtown years ago, when I was just getting started at this. When we all were. And when there *was* a downtown. I thought a lot of her."

"Most people did."

"You among them, I hope."

She turned her head abruptly to meet my eyes. Glasses swung at the end of their cord as breasts swayed and came to rest inside a bone-colored silk jumper. One hand, veins close to the surface, crept into view atop the desk. Signals everywhere.

"Here, I'll show you."

I followed her through mazes that would put Charlie and Algernon at their collective best to shame, trying hard not to focus on skirt, buttocks and taut calves before me. We came to rest, like the head of Orpheus, in the snag of an L-shaped desk lodged north-by-northwest, smack against a coral reef of bookshelves. Desktop all but bare, memos tacked up in perfect rows, half an inch between them on the horizontal, two on the vertical. But when I pulled open the top drawer, there it was, barely contained: the world's chaos.

"Her mother's daughter," I said.

I'd rummaged through half a dozen unmarked folders and envelopes stuffed with bits of inscribed paper when Ms. LeBlanc leaned against my shoulder to pose another nonquestion: "You're looking for something specific."

I was, and, all things considered, didn't mind her knowing, though I wasn't sure how far onto that particular bridge I wanted to walk just yet. She forestalled my having to decide.

"The job entails a bit more than answering phones and being able to plow one's way through the morass of grant applications, Lewis. My degree is in law. When I found I was unable to practice, that I couldn't in good conscience accommodate myself to the system—a child of the Sixties after all, though mostly I was absent from and oblivious of the era's great events, being too busy with my studies to take much notice—I began casting about for alternatives. This is what I came up with."

"You're lucky."

She nodded. "Most of us never find a place we fit. And I'm good at this. Good enough to suspect that Alouette has been receiving threats, for instance."

"Oh."

"And to assume that's what you're looking for."

"How did you know?"

"I didn't. Only suspected it."

"But you never talked to her about it."

"She never talked about it with me. It was her place to bring it up, not mine. Threats are a commonplace in our world, with what we do. We receive them all the time, in every kind of package—overt, implied, physical, psychological. Face to face in the heat of confrontations. Over phones at three in the morning. Downstream from bureaucrats in suits and cell phones and upstream from clients lugging their few precious wordly goods about in plastic bags or shopping carts."

"You thought the threats were routine, then. Not serious." Now I was doing it. Nonquestions.

"In their way they all are. I do think Alouette failed to take them seriously." Valerie LeBlanc leaned back onto the window ledge, which canted her hips forward, pushing belly and thighs tight against the front of her skirt. She did this with the air of someone wholly unaware of her body, the effects it engendered. "Part of it's that she doesn't take herself seriously, you know."

"She works hard."

"Harder than almost anyone else around here. But that also serves to direct her away from herself. Sound like anyone you know?"

"Sounds like everyone I know. Pardon me, miss, but your Sixties are showing."

"They usually do, however careful I am to tuck them in. Nineteen-ninety-six, the year he died, my father was still ranting about murderous, inhuman Japs. Talk about holding grudges. And people say Americans have no sense of history! So maybe I'm doomed to the same? Stuck in place like all those people with lacquered hair and leisure suits on the religious channel, flat and lifeless as pressed flowers. History's torpedoes streaming towards me in silence." She pushed off the window ledge. "Come on, let's peek."

I followed back through the maze to her desk. "Mind you," she said, "peeking's nowhere near as exciting as it used to be."

"Things get that way at our age."

She sat before her computer. "They don't have to." Fingers rippled on the keyboard as though with a will of their own, the very figure of the socialist agenda, each finger acting independently though in concert, courting the common good.

"At some level, always, we're just looking for the secret stuff. Not much difference there between Molly Bloom and Sally Raphael."

Fingers went on as she spoke. I thought of H. G. Wells's Martians stilting towards London, soldiers in blue peering down from the hills over Vicksburg, young men in Sopwith Camels who cast an eye on life, on death, flew on.

"This whole thing," she said, nodding towards the

computer, "is a morass, an ethical slough. I can punch in and find out instantly who's left messages on my machine, cruise business prospects and keep up with friends, have the world's news at my fingertips. But I can also, with the flick of that same finger, call up a list of sex offenders and their current addresses. These are people, mind you, who've served their time, paid their debt. People who, according to every tenet of a Constitution we go on and on claiming to be so proud of, are fundamentally protected."

Menus and directories bloomed on the screen, gave way to others, in a constant wash.

"Most days I bemoan that loudly. Decry, despise and disavow it." She stopped, fingers still, and read what she had, then clacked a few more keys. Columns of icons and keywords filled the screen. "Here's a file Alouette had tucked away in a private folder. Swept under the rug, as it were. Correspondence, mostly. And mostly electronic, from the look of it."

"Can I get a —"

But she'd already pushed the eject button, and was handing me a disk.

"Thanks."

"You're welcome. I hope it helps." She smiled. "Hate to invade someone's privacy for nothing. Maybe you'll let me know?"

Valerie LeBlanc replaced her glasses. Mission accomplished, good deeds done. No one would take her for the hero she was, now. Back to the workaday world.

Three hours and spare change later, I was sitting at a rear table in Tender Buttons, a converted drugstore where the food is great if profoundly idiosyncratic even by New Orleans standards. Service, on the other hand, might best be described as postmodern: sketchy, nonsequential and difficult to follow, forever self-conscious and oddly parodic as though in some inde-cipherable way alluding to other things entirely, say yak-raising or kazoo artistry.

Many of the entries from Alouette's computer, lacking referents or perspective, proved utterly indeci-pherable. Others had to do with various projects at work and appeared to be of no more than utilitarian interest. There was a file of personal letters and e-mail messages, another of (I think) references to newspa-per and magazine articles. But the one that caught my attention had been identified simply as GOK—Alou-ette's code, I recognized, for an intellectual shrug, God Only Knows—and I sat thinking about it as the waiter brought my catfish *au beurre noir* and grit cakes stud-ded with bits of bright habanero pepper, side of white asparagus, and vanished to reappear at irregular inter-vals, bursting suddenly upon the scene to linger there like a declaimed quote, or shuttling up all but unno-ticed, superfluous as a footnote.

The GOK file was a hodgepodge of lists, passages from novels and self-help books, advertising slogans, obituaries, cross sections of classified ads, altogether the most eclectic jumble of disparate things heaped up in a single place that I'd ever come across, a tour through America's waste lots and past its false, ruined faces, a landfill of used-up words, expended cartridges of old thoughts clattering to the floor. One list com-prised science-fiction titles.

"The Education of Drusilla Strange"
A Fabulous, Formless Darkness
To Walk the Night
The Man Who Fell to Earth
A Mirror for Observers

Another juxtaposed mysteries by Margery Allingham, Jonathan Latimer and Patricia Highsmith (provoca-

tive *n* added, one presumes in all innocence, to Ms.
Highsmith's given name), movies from the era of such
actors as Broderick Crawford, Richard Carlson and
Robert Mitchum, and TV shows like *I Led Three Lives*
and (with painstaking documentation of each individual episode) *The Prisoner*. One contained a long-
winded though rather breathless review of Donald
Westlake's Richard Stark novels from an alternative
magazine in the Midwest, another several excerpts
from Millay's *Collected Poems* and Adrienne Rich's
The Fact of a Doorframe. A publisher's flyer for a new
translation of *I'm Not Stiller* had been scanned in.

Messages everywhere.

Somehow I hadn't been altogether surprised to
find my own first novel, *The Old Man*, listed there.
Over coffee I sat thinking of that novel's dedication,
to David: *Non enim possunt militares pueri dauco ex-
ducier*. The sons of military men can't be raised on
carrots. Now here I was looking for others, shadows,
with my own son gone missing—out in the world
somewhere, as Buster Robinson and four or five gen-
erations of bluesmen put it. LaVerne would have had
something to say about that. So for that matter would
almost everyone else. Probably, if he knew, even my
waiter, who *ibid*'d by long enough to refill my coffee
and drop a check, albeit the wrong one, on my table.

"What's the *F* for?" I asked when, outwaited so
to speak, at length he returned. I'll read anything.
F. Prokov.

"F? Oh. The name tag, you mean. Not mine. I'm
filling in for my roommate, has a part in a new play.
My name's Alaine. Like Elaine but with an *A*."

As we got the check straightened out and, finally,
paid, I showed great control in refraining from com-
plimenting him on just how well he fit in with the
general waitstaff. Definitely in the groove. They'd
probably wind up asking him to stay on.

Outside the bar next door, near a crape myrtle whose limbs had crossed like fingers then intergrown to the point of having no separate existence, a young man and woman stood talking. "But honey, you *know* what I mean," the man said as I came out of Tender Buttons. He looked into her face as though he had himself forgotten what he meant but thought he might find reminders of it there. Farther along, half a block or so, I paused to marvel at a dogwood's spectacular involucres, as though huge thumbs had pressed each flower into place, then before a yard whose chain-link fence was interlaced with pinwheels of every size and color, dozens of them, all whirring gaily away.

Following upon several hours of sunlight, New Orleans had again gone gray, as if the city had been turned inside out or some anti-city been unearthed, bleak where the original was bright. Purple-gray bellies of clouds hung overhead. Wind whipped about in the trees and beat its fist against the sides of buildings. Lines from a poem I'd read years ago came to me:

> *Tell me again why, at the edge*
> *of the world, the wind screams.*

Across the street, someone had stacked magazines at curbside for pickup after sorting them into bundles and wrapping each bundle with twine. Now a man perhaps my age in layers of ragged clothing sat tearing apart each bundle and picking through, placing his selections carefully in a new pile beside him. Wind threw back exposed covers like bedclothes, ripped through pages. It would be a long winter. There was little enough a man could do about that, but he might at least stock up on reading matter.

About the same time I came across that poem in a magazine, I also read a book of short stories by one of the young Southern writers then briefly fashionable.

Something troubled me about the stories, some residue I couldn't quite define or throw off. After a few days I picked the book up again, and soon had it: each story ended with a man walking back to his hotel alone or standing at a window looking out. This was in the early Nineties, and I was living, more adrift than usual, in a constant shuffle back and forth between furnished rooms and LaVerne's. David had vanished, I thought for good, leaving behind a few moments' silence on my answering machine. Putting in his own time (I imagined) walking back to dreary rooms and standing by windows. Watching the world pass by just out of reach, acceptance, participation, understanding.

We always have to understand, don't we, the two of us? That's another thing I must get away from.

Closer to home I passed a neighborhood grill and looked in to see a waiter who at first appeared to have been in a terrible accident, his arm a clutch of raw meat. But it was merely bacon he held, draped over the arm (much as in movies fancy waiters hold towels over their arms) preparatory to cooking.

Five or six blocks further along, a homeless man had deposited his jumble of bags beneath a tree in an empty lot and lay knees up among them as though reclining in a field of high grass or flowers. Person and possessions, man and baggage, were indistinguishable, equally still, equally serene, in perfect lack of expectation.

11

THING is, I walked out of the building and the cops were standing there waiting for me.

There was this sort of gate at the entryway, and I froze just outside it. The gate was cast iron and once had something written on it in art deco script, but now only two letters were left, an *L* and an *I*, spaced far apart.

"Don't s'pose you live here," one of them, the older one, said.

"Don't rightly see how anyone could. Back home our barns're better'n this shithole."

I held both hands up in plain view.

"You been drinkin', boy?"

I shook my head. Best, always, to say as little as possible. That was true back home, even more true here in the city. I'd been in New Orleans a year or so at the time, and was learning fast.

"Here to buy dope, then."

"No sir."

"Damn. You're one polite nigger, ain't you?"

They walked me over to the squad between them. I made to lean against it and spread my feet.

"No need for that," the older one said. He smiled. The smile reminded me of alligator gars into whose mouths we'd jam sticks, then watch them sink and fight their way back to the surface and sink again till they died. "You been up to the third floor by any chance?"

I shook my head.

"You sure 'bout that."

I nodded.

"'Cause there's a man up there makes his living selling dope to kids. We don't like that much."

"No sir."

"Maybe you don't either."

"No sir."

"Maybe if we went up there right now we'd find he's given up his former occupation."

"I wouldn't know anything about that, officer."

"No . . . no, of course you wouldn't." A car sped by on the street. He followed it with his eyes, then looked back. "I haven't seen you before, have I?"

"No sir."

"New in town?"

"Right new, yes sir."

"Got family here?"

"No sir."

"Heading back home soon, then?"

"I 'spect so, yes sir."

"So I won't be seeing you again."

I shook my head.

"Good."

"You're free to go," the younger one said. "He's free to go, right?"

"Free as he's gonna git, anyway." They had a good laugh over that.

"Thank you, officers. You take care now, you hear?"
And I walked away.

Away from apartment 321, where Harry Soames lay fouling pale blue tile with his blood.

"What the fuck, let 'em kill each other off," the younger cop said behind me.

Two months after I'd come down from Arkansas, I met Angie at a Burger King on Carrollton. You could get a dinner there, burger, fries, drink, for about two dollars. She didn't have it. And though I didn't have much more myself, I sprang for her meal. I wasn't so hardened back then, I hadn't seen a lot.

We lived together for six, seven weeks. Didn't take me long to find out Angie was an addict. But long as she got her stuff, she was good. And slowly over those days and weeks, without giving it a name or thinking much about it, I was falling in love with her.

Then one night—I'd started doing collections, which tends to be nighttime work—I came home and found Angie stretched out on the couch. She looked perfectly at rest. Some detective show was on TV, light from the screen washing over her. She'd popped corn and the full bowl sat beside her on the coffee table, along with a full glass of lemonade. She was dead.

12

Years ago, in one or another of my hospital stays, LaVerne brought me a crackly old recording of Negro poetry. She'd come across it, on a New York City label more often given to Southern field recordings or folk music by aged Trotskyites and scruffily dressed suburban youngsters, with the occasional klezmer, fado or polka disk thrown in for good measure, at a client's home. Following my initial, instinctive repulsion, I'd fallen in thrall to those voices, to Langston Hughes's "Night comes slowly, black like me" and the poem just before, which described a Southern lynching. That one in particular I listened to again and again, riding the tone arm as it rose and spun and fell, words and images spilling from the grooves; till finally the weight of it all, shoveled from the record's trenches, settled onto me. In subsequent years, without ever intending to, I'd begun collecting such poems. They'd push in past my feet as I opened the door and not be put back out. Then one day, browsing a ramshackle antique store in the Faubourg Marigny, I swung open the top of an old school desk to find, atop a packet of letters tied with string, a postcard dated Jun 3 1931. The message, in glorious Palmer loops and dips, read *Geo. and family doing good. Yesterday we took ourselves out to these mounds that were bilt hundreds of yrs ago by no one knows who. Just these humps, like they'd done buried an elephant. Home soon. Yr wife, Dorothy.* Much of the ink had faded, until only the outline of letters, like dry husks, remained. I turned the postcard over. On its front, a young black man hung from one middling limb of a pecan tree. All the limbs went up at sharp angles, as though in a rush towards sky. The man hung there, an afterthought, trying to tug this single branch back down. The rope about his neck was obscenely thick, thick as a man's arm. His feet were bare and so bloated with pooled blood that they looked like melons. Beneath him, in the tree's shade, a group of whites sat looking into the camera with cups raised.

As I walked back up into the Quarter towards Canal, past flotillas of tourists, shop owners hosing down sidewalks, mule-drawn carriages and delivery vans that looked as though they'd sustained artillery attacks, things began coming together in heart and head at odd angles. Half a block from Jackson Square I wheeled about and went back, bought the postcard for five dollars. Two weeks later I proposed *Strange Fruit, Strange Flowers* to my publisher. Had I written it, the book would have been an extended essay on the art and literature of lynching; it would have been also, leaving aside the unpublished autobiography, my only nonfiction book. It sold on prospectus the first time out to a major publisher for what my agent called "a respectable advance"—approximately what I'd made for all my novels to date combined. Then a long odyssey as editors came and went, book's file staggering from desk to desk, carried home to Brooklyn on the F train, left behind at the Cheyenne Diner but recovered, correspondence outgrowing prospectus and contract like weeds taking over a vacant lot.

"I had no idea," I'd say to Clare, weeks into the thing, "how difficult this would be, or how different. Writing a novel's never easy. No way around putting in the time and sweat. And you never really know what you're doing. There's a stack of lumber and nails you've got to turn into walls somehow. Find a place for doorways, windows and sills and figure out some way to put them in. But for all that, it's more like building a tree house, tacking on a porch. *This* is like remodeling your bathroom: walls a smelly map of mildew and stain, floors torn out, reeking, jagged pipes everywhere. And nothing fits anything else."

Those first weeks and for some time after, as the book in its pod (I thought) grew a body, face, hands, I'd been a faithful carpenter. Turned up at local archives and libraries day after day with such regularity that the guards and I came to know one another. Sometimes I'd join them, bearing cups of carryout coffee, on the back steps before opening. Drink and chat a few minutes, then go inside and lay out legal pads, pens, Post-It notes, index cards, retrieve books held for me overnight under the counter, settle in at a table.

Once during an afternoon break I stood outside with a guard named Jean. Well past fifty, body unbowed and unslowed by time, features smooth as stone, he dismounted the bus each morning with shirt laundered and starched, trousers pressed to a crease that could slice butter. Half a block over, in the square before City Hall, long folding tables had been set up to feed the homeless and indigent. I looked from orderly queues awaiting allotments of stew, bread and applesauce, to the motel across the street where thirty-plus years ago a man named Terence Gully had

clambered to the roof with a .44-caliber Magnum rifle, a duffel bag full of ammunition, and four genera-
tions of racial pain.

A man about the same age as my companion,
wearing ancient khakis, Madras sportcoat and two or
three shirts, all of them in tatters, walked across Poy-
dras from downtown. With him was a girl of perhaps
twelve, his daughter, perhaps, the two of them to every
appearance living together on the streets. Each bore a
backpack, blankets tied into bedrolls and swung under
one arm. The girl's clothes were as hodgepodge as his:
oversize men's jeans, sweatshirt from which cute paw-
in-paw kittens had long ago faded, grimy John Deere
gimme cap. But as they came closer, I saw her face.
Base and powder, liner and eye shadow, a touch of
rouge, pale lipstick.

"Pretty girl. Got one 'bout that age myself," Jean
said beside me. He put out his cigarette on the sole of
a steel-toed shoe, held it cradled in one hand for dis-
posal. "Had, anyway. Wife up and left me two, three
weeks ago."

"I'm sorry."

Jean shrugged. "Prob'ly for the best."

After he'd gone back in, I stood watching father
and daughter inch along the line, plates slowly filling.
I thought about parents and children, about David
and Alouette, Terence Gully, the young man hanging
from that pecan tree on the postcard. Had he had
children? Not much more than a child himself. Another of America's horde of invisible men. They pass
through life a shadow, leaving no impression. Never
in his life would that young black man have had occa-
sion to be photographed. Or to have been entered in
any record beyond statistics of birth and death. Now
there he hung for all time.

What research taught me was that such postcards
were once common. They'd existed by the hundreds,

handed across counters like advertising circulars, stuffed into bags of flour and patent medicine, spread on hallway tables in rooming houses, propped up in shop windows. That fall I traveled to a small town in Pennsylvania whose university library had amassed a major collection, possibly the only collection, of these cards. I went through the lot, made copious notes and photocopies, had dinner, half a dozen weak drinks and lunch the next day with the collection's curator. An elderly gentleman with pinkish hair and eyes, he spoke with authority and passion while seeming at the same time apologetic, even embarrassed, by his calling. Dressed in the first seersucker suit I'd seen outside New Orleans (though without the accompanying bow tie), he had the bearing, weather-beaten skin and accent of an Alabama laborer, and a Ph.D. from Princeton. Back home, I haunted Tulane's Special Collections, the Amistad, Xavier.

For all my best intentions and time accrued, alas, that book soon went the way of others, left unfinished, never truly begun. Yet somehow poems still found their way to me. Days before I walked out on teaching, in the course of preparing a lecture on comic novelists, I'd come across one by Charles Henri Ford in a book on Peter De Vries.

> I, Rainy Betha,
> from the top-branch of race-hatred look
>   at you.
> My limbs are bound, though boundless the
>   bright sun
> like my bright blood which had to run
> into the orchard that excluded me:
> now I climb death's tree.
> The pruning-hooks of many mouths
> cut the black-leaved boughs.
> The robins of my eyes hover where
> sixteen leaves fall that were a prayer:

sixteen mouths are open wide;
the minutes like black cherries
drop from my shady side.

That confusion, the near-gnostic fusion of two lives, tree and hanged person becoming one, seems to me perfect, as does the poem's fine concluding image, *minutes like black cherries drop from my shady side.*

Newly returned from my recon of Alouette's workplace and bibliophilic dinner at Tender Buttons, I sat at the kitchen table in LaVerne's old house thinking about David, with Ford's poem, especially that last line, ticking in my head. Deborah had left a note on the refrigerator, in a space we'd agreed to keep clear of the archaeological litter of old messages, scrawled drawings, unpaid bills, clippings and photos that scaled the rest: *Casting tonight, may be late, VERY late, love you.* That had made me remember another note encountered years ago (*Home soon*) on a picture postcard. Then the poem.

Back when I was writing more or less regularly and able to delude myself I might more or less make a living at it, I'd always kept notepads within reach. Now I found one on a shelf beneath an alluvium of receipts and unopened mail, food coupons long expired, blotched handwritten recipes, turned-back sections from the *Times-Picayune* or *New York Times,* half a paperback copy of *Huckleberry Finn,* and a Loompanics catalog. When I slammed the pad's edge against the table, dust, cat hair and dessicated insect parts fell away. Further down in the compost heap I found a skittery ballpoint.

Your faces turn up to me, those I know and those I'll never know, there's little difference. All your sad mouths and hungry eyes and wayward feet, all your stories waiting to be told. But who will tell them now? This gentle sun is high. It waits for me. Minutes like black cherries drop from my side.

Deborah came home well past midnight to find me still there at the table, sheaves of pages pushed to the back, against the wall. We talked awhile distractedly, she went up to bed, I brewed a pot of strong coffee, made sandwiches, and went on scribbling. Just after six that morning—by this time I'd moved out onto the porch—I heard her descending stairs, calling after me. Moments later, wrapped in a blanket, she came out. We sat together watching dawn spread its skirt above the trees.

"You're writing again," she said after a while.

"For the moment."

"A book?"

"Could be."

"That's good, Lew." She looked tired. "Kettle's on for tea, if you want some. I could fix biscuits."

"I'm fine."

"You sure?"

I nodded. "Up early, huh?"

"Still wired."

We sat quietly. Lights came on in upstairs bedrooms, bathrooms and downstairs kitchens. Marcie waved as she got into her car and backed out of the driveway on her way to Baptist, where she worked critical care.

"How'd the casting go?"

"Good. Better than good, really. You forget how much talent there is. Most everything's in place, I think."

"Great."

"I keep telling myself that. Trying to see around the elephant: that it's only a start."

Out in the kitchen, the kettle began whistling.

"This kid came in," Deborah said. "He's fifteen, sixteen, maybe. Shorts hanging down around his calves, shirt two or three sizes too large, unlaced British Knights. Hair like tumbleweed. No experience, no photo, no résumé. Walks in a slump, like he might collapse, boneless, any minute. God knows what got him there. Or what prompted me to give him a shot. But I told him I'd like him to read from one of the choruses. He looks at me and says okay. Picks the book up, looks at it once, and puts it down. Then he starts in. And I realize he's got it, words, rhythm, the whole thing, just from that quick glance. But he's not doing it straight. He's jamming the part, spinning out this weird reggae/hip-hop thing from Aristophanes' words. And it's just right, incredibly right.

"I had chills, Lew. Everyone did." She stood, shrugging the blanket up around her. "You particularly desperate for coffee or tea?"

"No."

"Then the hell with it, I'm going back to bed. Join me?"

"I want to read through this first."

I listened to her mount the stairs, heard the radio come on, toilet flush, water run into the sink. Looked at the pages I'd shuffled more or less into order.

A black man is about to be hung on the oak beneath which he played as a child, often as not with the children of white neighbors and overseers. Latterly he's become a kind of minstrel, a guitarist and singer, a storyteller. He looks out at all these other faces and something suddenly fills him, something he doesn't understand, can't name, has never felt before. He begins telling jokes, riffing on his fate. The entire novel, 125 pages, takes place in the moments before he drops.

There are altogether too many explanations, Peter De Vries writes, too many systems. They cancel one another out, till only the *why* remains, the question mark we can't rid ourselves of: that fishhook in the heart. Trying to understand, we cry Let there be light—and only the dawn breaks.

Researching, I'd found in Xavier's archives the vestige of a black newspaper published around the turn of the century, documenting community life in a town whose black population essentially had been shipped north to serve white male college students. No record of who might have edited, written or printed the newspaper: all invisible men. Only this microfilm image of the front page survived. Stories were continued to inside pages that no longer exist.

13

ONE o'clock of a blurry afternoon. Clouds dragging low in the sky, like the bellies of middle-aged men in bars and bowling alleys. Don has something unidentifiable, fried chicken maybe, or soggy brown cauliflower, on the plate before him. I've had three hours' sleep and can't even remember dressing to get here. Blur reigns.

"Thanks for coming, Lew. I need you to tell me how crazy this is."

"Just as soon as you spoon all that up. Be a brave boy, now." I thought of Virgil, a kid from the sticks like myself. Can't imagine why. Because Deborah's wrestle with Greek comedy had body-slammed me into some classical mood? "After which, I'm your man. Crazy being something I know."

What I didn't know was where the hell this was going. I looked out over the plain of starched sheet, pale face, across jagged peaks of lumpish brown rising from the flatland, past the forkful of same entering his mouth. Soft light in the windows of his eyes, self there inside groping its way along dim corridors, bumping into doorways. Never a man to seek another's sanction. And not quite the Don I was used to.

"What do you think of Derick, Lew?"

"Kid that shot you."

"Yeah. Jeeter."

I shrugged. "No reason to give it much thought. Should I have? He seems like a good enough kid, I guess, underneath it all. Maybe you do have to scratch deeper than with most."

"Yeah. Maybe. And maybe you scratch deep enough, we're all pretty much the same. Derick and I get along, you know? Could be there's some kind of real connection. Who the fuck knows?"

Don was one of the few cops who managed not to be changed, violated, by what he did. Day after day, year after year, he sat at his ancient, dented, yellow desk with the highest murder rate in the country rising around him like floodwaters, journalists snapping at ankles and knees and city-hall hacks thinking they'd live large by swallowing him headfirst, events of his own life coruscating down like acid rain; and still he'd take time to go meet some youth coming out of lockup and give him a ride home, drop by and leave off groceries with the family of a man he'd sent up.

"It's not like he has anywhere to go, Lew. Or anything waiting for him there if he did. You know as well as I do what his future looks like. Scratching by, one continuous hustle, the occasional demeaning job if he's lucky. Cheap room when he can afford it, the street when he can't, which'll be most of the time. Till eventually he tries another grab, and—if not that time, then the next—he gets taken down. At which point he's in the system for good."

"Meaning for bad."

"Always. A career con once told me it's like having concrete slowly poured around you. You move around less and less. Finally you don't move at all."

Don pushed tray and table away. They came to a swaying stop, seeming somehow to vibrate a degree or two out of sync with the world about us. Neither of us had ever quite fit, either. Just that sometimes, here and there, cycles would coincide. You learn to slip past closing doors, make your way among the world's pauses and stammers. Don stared at grease and glycerin-like brown smears left behind.

"Well, *that* was certainly interesting."

"I ever mention you're the kind of man on whom nothing is wasted?"

"Right, Lew. I ever mention how just because I'm a cop you think I'm not gonna know when you quote Henry James?"

"Most reviewers don't."

"Hey. Not their fault. They haven't had the advantage of repeatedly getting drunk with you, after all, hearing the same damn shit again and again."

"Good point."

"How're they gonna know where all that stuff comes from? LaVerne used to tell me how she'd read your latest book and remember back to when you guys had gone to some restaurant you were describing, or to a concert close enough to one in the book that she knew that's where it came from."

In the corridor outside, a comet streamed by: doctor on rounds, house staff of interns and residents, straggling tail of med students. Lab coats flapped all about; pockets crammed with guidebooks, rulers, rubber-capped hammers and stethoscopes, when they came to a stop, settled like trucks pulling up at a landfill. Various beepers sounded.

"I'm thinking about asking him to come home with me, Lew. Derick, I mean."

"I see. And you've talked this over with Jeanette, of course."

"Kind of."

"Meaning you haven't."

"She knows."

"No she doesn't, Don." Out the window, a phalanx of birds pulsed across the sky. Clouds moved in the opposite direction, so that the birds appeared to be moving at furious speed. They were, I thought, a caret, copyediting sky: insert horizon here. "She may suspect it, sense it. But she doesn't *know* until you tell her."

"You're right. But we've talked about this—haven't talked about much else lately, when you come right down to it. How Derick's life has gone, how it's likely to go. She understands he hasn't had much of a chance so far."

Birds having passed from the window's frame, a Southwest Airlines plane, tiny, iconlike, nosed in to replace them.

"Talk to her, Don. She loves you."

"She does, doesn't she?"

"What about Derick himself? What does he say about all this?"

"I'll have to let you know."

Crowding a cursory knock at the door, Santos stepped into the room. Coat, shirt and slacks looked as though they'd been stuffed into pillowcases for storage and recently fetched out; his tie was bent back on itself like a dog-eared page. A faint reek of garlic, vintage sweat, stale smoke and bourbon came off him.

"Captain."

"Tony. Up and at it already," Don said.

Santos shook his head. "Still. I got home long enough to pour two fingers of bourbon and drink the first joint of one of them. Then the beeper went off."

"Short night."

"For sure. You told me I'd better get used to them."

"Long finger of the law. Forever poking at you."

"More like a thumb lodged securely up my butt."

"Smile. Fake 'em out. Maybe they'll think you like it. Maybe you'll even get to. It could happen."

"Fuck that." Santos looked around. Wondering if this was the way he'd wind up, too? If this was what it might come down to, all those years of white nights and bleary mornings, hours at the desk waiting for something to break, while slowly hearts turned hard all around and the hemorrhoids you sat on grew to the size of ostrich eggs? "Didn't know Griffin was here."

"Brought the massuh breakfast," I said.

"I'll just bet you did. Hitched your mule to that pickaninny post outside, no doubt."

"Just like we knew it was you right away. Heard the clack of those stacked heels."

"I assume you want something, Tony," Don said, "and didn't just take a wrong turn at the coffeepot downtown."

"Might be better if Griffin waited outside, Captain."

"Lot of people have felt that way in the past. What're you gonna do? Here he is."

"Yeah. Here he is." Santos's eyes, unreadable as ever, flicked from Don's to mine and back. "Call came in last night from a phone booth, anonymous. Squad responded and found a body. This was down in the hub, what they're calling the industrial district these days. Where all those apartment complexes went up a few years back, the ones no one moved into. No one that paid, anyway. Block after block of double-gated entrances, intercoms, internal corridors, skylights. Empty as seashells."

New Orleans has never had much luck with gentrification. Every few years the city grasps at some straw it's become certain will save it: the 1984 World's Fair, gambling casinos a decade or so later, or converting the blasted, abandoned ruins of downtown

warehouses, on a New York model, into apartments.
But the city always winds up in worse shape than before, deeper in debt and ever more desperate, its
dreams like Matilda in the old Harry Belafonte song
having took the money and run Ven'zuela.

"Squad pulls up. Earl Jackson, Tyra McIlvane.
He's been on the job a month or two, barely cleared
ride-along. She's got almost a year in, making her an
old hand by today's standards, way they come and go.
The gate, they finally figure, is jammed shut, chewing
gum or something like that in the lock, it looks secure
but gives when they shove. They go up slowly, door to
door. Garbage covers the stairs, sacks from McDonald's, pizza cartons, quart bottles of Old Milwaukee,
crack vials, cheap wine, lumpy, burned-out mattresses. On the third floor, in what might have been a
choice apartment looking out over Lee Circle, only it's
not, it never got to be that and never will, they find
the body.

"Been there a long time, they figure. Most of the
features are gone and the whole thing's puffed up like
the bad spot on a tire, about to let go. Unbelievably this
guy still has a wallet in his pocket. There's close to sixty
dollars in there. No driver's license, no credit cards.
And a social security card issued to David Griffin."

"Lewis," Dr. Bijur said.

"We know one another," I told Santos, who had
started to introduce us.

"You . . . were a great help . . . to Walsh."

"We do what we can."

"Some . . . of us do."

The last time I saw her was when Don's son Danny
killed himself. We'd stood together beside the old
clawfoot tub he lay in, half afloat, half submerged.
Danny had overdosed and backed up the overdose by

tying a plastic bag around his head the way the Hem-
lock Society people said to. Blood vessels in his eyes
had burst, making them look like road maps with
nothing but interstates.

At that time, years back, Dr. Bijur looked, herself,
to be barely hanging on, living off Atrovent and Al-
buterol inhalers in lieu of air. She still was. I hoped to
hell she got a professional discount on the things.

"As I told . . . Santos," she went on, stringing
words on double fenceposts of pauses for breath and
hits off her inhalers, "we're not . . . sure what's happened."

With each breath her shoulders lifted to help
draw in air and her head thrust upward like a turtle's
to add that extra tiny pull. Her ankles were round as
soccer balls. Cracked everywhere, her skin had gone
gray and dry as parchment from constant steroid use.
Back in Arkansas, creeks and rivers would recede,
leaving behind mudflats that, baked in the sun,
looked much like her skin.

"Someone could have taken a carving knife to
him, from the look of it," Santos said, "then followed
up with a vegetable peeler. Mostly, the features are
gone. Ears, toes. Not much skin left, either. Your son's
been gone how long?"

"Just over a week."

"No word from him?"

"None."

"No idea where he might have gone?"

"Not really."

"And no recent change in habits? Suddenly talka-
tive, stops talking altogether maybe, starts staying to
himself?"

"I know the drill, Santos."

"Sure you do. No one new in his life, then?
Woman, male friend, lost parent?"

I shook my head. "I assumed he'd gone back to

the streets. *Descendre dans la rue,* as the French put it. Doesn't transfer well to English, but it's what the French have always done—1789, 1830, 1871 or last week, it's all pretty much the same—when the world starts weighing on them."

"He's got a history of this kind of thing, then. Dropping out. Disappearing."

I nodded.

A morgue assistant in dreadlocks that looked as though they'd been pressed between hot rocks made his way through the minefield of gurneys, found one and, bent like a surfer over his board, rolled it towards us. When he pulled back the rough sheet, Santos and Dr. Bijur looked up at him. A young woman's body lay there, face gray, lips and breasts pale and translucent as wax. He checked the toe tag.

"Sorry, man," he said. "Wrong citizen."

Moments later, he trucked another gurney and rider down the waves. From size and general build, the body under the sheet easily could be David's, I thought. But when Smashed Dreadlocks pulled back the cover, the world you and I live in day to day went flying away. What lay underneath looked like a skinned deer, a *Gray's Anatomy* dissection showing muscle, sinews and tendons, flesh that peculiar maroon color. Most of one eye was left. And the eye wasn't David's.

I told them so. "What happened?"

"First we thought some kind of compulsive, serial killer thing," Santos said.

"Too many bad . . . movies." This from Dr. Bijur.

"Yeah, but how're you *not* gonna think that. Just look at this poor son of a bitch. Some kid practicing peeling grapes, you think?"

Back home, in the hill country not far from where I was raised, poor folk lived off squirrels they nailed to trees then skinned in a single long tear. The meat went into skillets for frying and into pots for stew. The skins stayed behind on trees. Dozens of them, hundreds finally, ringing the homestead.

"Not much . . . I could put my finger on . . . a hunch. . . . Kind of thing happens . . . you do this all these years."

When she stopped to rest from that last headlong plunge, I realized that Santos and I were breathing hard ourselves. If this had been a musical, all the bodies on gurneys under sheets would start chugging right along with us.

"We have someone on call . . . for situations like . . . this. Professor at LSU . . . came right down. New York . . . one or two other major cities've . . . got them on staff . . . full-time."

Santos and I exchanged glances.

"You told me on the phone it was bugs," he said.

Taking a hit off one of her inhalers, Dr. Bijur decided it was empty. She tossed it backhand towards one of several tall galvanized cans sitting about (best not to think what might be in there), then started rummaging in the soft plastic cooler slung over her shoulder for a replacement. The discarded one fell short by a yard and hit the floor spinning. Santos walked over, picked it up, sank it.

"You're supposed to float . . . the damn things. They tip over, whatever . . . they're still good. Like we aren't going to know . . . when they don't . . . work anymore?"

Her eyes went wide with the fresh (concentrated?) hit.

"Greevy's a forensic . . . entomologist. Roaches were hard at work . . . he says. Man'd only been there . . . two, three days, not . . . weeks, like we'd thought."

"And my son's wallet? How'd that get there?"

Dr. Bijur shrugged her shoulders. At first I didn't take it for what it was; it looked like all her other struggles for breath.

"He doesn't drive and . . . there's no . . . bus . . . for

a while. Bill'd probably . . . be out at the site . . . if you wanted to go by."

One of those typical New Orleans cul-de-sacs, city's ancient soul pushing up through layers of attempts at refurbishment, this long-unused lot in the crook of old buildings extended half a block before it ended at a wall of cinder block serving no discernible purpose. Yet even here, on this bare, abandoned island, in the shade of automobile tires, shopping carts, shattered wine and antiseptic bottles, sacks of garbage bleached gray and dry as driftwood, life went on.

Dr. Greevy sat on the overturned ceramic tumbler of a Sixties washing machine. The console stood alongside, *Large load*, *Normal*, *Warm/cold* dialed in— for how many years now? Green shoots ran out from beneath the tumbler. Knees apart with elbows propped on them, Greevy held the last two inches of a po-boy in both hands. Sauce and part of a meatball ejected when he took a bite. He chewed once or twice and swallowed.

"You'd be Griffin."

I nodded.

"It wasn't your son, was it?"

"No."

"Didn't think so." He finished off the po-boy, wiped hands on the backs of trouser legs. "Body was up there, third floor, but you know that. Not much to see. Anything likely to be of use to you, it probably rolled out of here with the body."

"I don't even know what I'm looking for."

"We never do. Count ourselves lucky if we're able to figure out so much as what direction to look in." He smiled. "Man had your son's wallet. Stands to reason you'd want to know what killed him, where he'd been—anything you can find out. It's a deep canyon, with only this foot-wide path up here on the rim. But it's what you have."

"And you're going to tell me that? What killed him, where he'd been?"

"Some of it, anyway. Like everything else, that depends mostly on luck. Give me a few days."

Greevy reached behind him. He'd tucked a bottle of Pearl back there, and in the interim a grasshopper had claimed it as perch. Slowly Greevy brought the bottle up close, until the two of them were eye to eye.

"It's really their world, you know."

Kiting out over fragments of brick, dropping at glide's end onto a grassy patch, the grasshopper took flight. Greevy sat looking after it.

"City has several dozen varieties of roach," he said at length. "All of them as distinct as individual human faces, many of them deriving from one specific area of the city. Not to mention the others. Fleas, mites, lice. Moths and ants. Or our best if most rapacious friends, flies. Not only different from one another, but vastly different in behavior, diet, where they lay their eggs, how the young develop, gestation period."

Greevy took a deep swig of beer and held the bottle out to me. What the hell. Here we were, casual scientists, two men of the world talking things over, trying to understand. I drank and passed the bottle back.

"Day or two, the samples I took will start hatching. From the eyes, mouth, wounds. I'll be able to tell you more then. Almost to the moment how long he'd been dead. What he'd been eating. What parts of the city he frequented."

The bottle shuttled back another time or two.

"Strange work you do," I said.

Though there'd been no bell, kids began spilling out onto streets from a school nearby, those with top grades, I assumed, let go early as reward. They took to bicycles and buses and looked impossibly young, part of the world's order and continuity. They fit.

One of them, though, twelve maybe, a girl with skin white as paper and coppery hair, stepped in front of us and stood there fiercely.

"What are you men doing?" she said.

Greevy ignored her.

"You've been sitting there watching, for a long time now. I saw you from inside, through the window. That's how it can start. I should call the police."

"We're just friends, miss," Greevy said, "catching up on things. Neither of us even knew there was a school nearby. Believe me, no harm's intended."

"Sure you are. You people *never* intend harm, do you? And this is where you usually meet, right? In the middle of a vacant lot."

"Miss. I'm sorry. I don't know what else I can tell you."

A bus pulled in at the stop across from the school. Our inquisitor's eyes went from us to the bus and back.

"Well—" She turned and ran for the bus, sprang aboard. We saw her face in the back window, still watching us, till the bus passed out of sight. Neither Greevy nor I spoke for a time.

"Had a son once myself," he said finally. "Long gone now."

"Divorce?"

"Death."

"I'm sorry."

"Yeah. Me too." He upended the empty bottle. A drop or two came out. "Boy was never right. Just couldn't get it together, and even when someone else'd pull it together for him, he couldn't keep it in the road. Something just got left out in the mix, you know. No one's fault. But no one should have to live like that, either. All I could think when I heard was, Good, he's not hurting anymore.

"It's all a gift, Griffin. All of it. You think maybe your son, wherever he is, knows that?"

"I think he does, yes."

"Good." After a moment he said, "So how do I get in touch, assuming I have something for you?"

I scribbled name, address and phone number on a sheet from my notebook, tore it out and handed it to him. It went haphazardly into a coat pocket, no surprise. Though from general appearance the coat had been in use for some time, the pocket was still sewn shut. He had to rip out stitches to get the paper in.

"Circle K up by the corner," he said. "Still have more than an hour before my ride shows up. You want, we could grab a quart of beer, a couple of dogs."

Fine idea, I said, just what I wanted, and we swung that way. But when we got there a tour bus sat across the street. Through storefront windows we could see streams of elderly folk clutching bags of chips and pretzels, bottles of orange juice, candy bars, souvenir pralines. Greevy and I ended up on the curb by a nearby Exxon station. NOPD cars came drifting past as kids schlepped home lumpy knapsacks, lunchboxes, Gameboys, Walkmen, form-fitted saxophone and French horn cases.

"They think it's Disneyland," Greevy said.

"Kids?"

"The tourists. Look at them. Like this is what they've been waiting for all along, what their lives've come down to, this pitiful bus ride with a package of Fritos and an adventure happening outside the window at the end. The kids know better. At least I hope to hell they do."

Listing right then left, a man with bandy legs approached us.

"Sonny Payne," he said. "How do you do. I'm

homeless and I'm hungry. If you don't have it, I understand, because I don't have it either. But if you do, anything you might see fit to pass on, a sandwich, a few
coins, a piece of fruit, will be appreciated. Thank you."

He stood there swaying, ticking it out. No response came, he'd move along, deliver the same
speech verbatim just down the line. Greevy, however,
pulled out his wallet and handed the man a ten.

"Thank you, sir."

"My son was on the streets for years." Greevy
passed the quart of Corona to me. One of the NOPD
cars slowed to check us out, then went on.

"I think it's against the law, our sitting out here
drinking," I told him.

"Yeah. Probably is." He took the bottle back and
drained it. "You up for one more?"

14

As I make my way home, traversing abandoned lots, shoulder-narrow alleys, car-beset stretches of St. Charles, Jackson and Prytania, darkness lays its hand on the city, gently at first, then ever more firmly. Portions of sunlight cling to the edges of buildings. Headlights and streetlights straggle on. In houses I pass, behind windows tall as a man, wood floors are held in place by antique dining tables, barrister's bookcases and overpadded chairs. In there, too, light falls: white light like cool pure water from chandeliers, light yellow and warm from table and floor lamps.

I turned onto Prytania, skirting a house that looked like any other save for a discreet metal sign hung from its eave: Anderssen Real Estate. I've probably walked past a hundred times without taking notice. A fortyish man wearing slacks and an open-neck white dress shirt still crisp from the morning's iron emerged, locked up, mounted a silver BMW and rode away. Almost immediately another man stepped around the low wall of cinder block separating this house's driveway from that of the next. He made for a niche tucked between house and wall beneath an overbite of roof and there unrolled his blanket, positioning himself on it and setting out with every aspect of ritual a well-used plastic bottle of water, cans of food, backpack, folded newspapers. Then began pulling off braces and supports. The crutch he'd had under his left arm. Neck brace padded with foam. Wrap-around knee support. Plastic form into which right foot and ankle had been strapped. Wrist splint with wide Velcro ties attached. Elastic elbow wrap. Some weird sympathetic magic—he wore these, none of it could happen to him? Or had he from whatever obscure motive—sympathy, instinct for salvage, pride of ownership—simply fished them from refuse bins at nearby Touro Infirmary, slowly accumulating, growing one might almost say, this exoskeleton within which he went about the world?

My own house of wooden floors, high ceilings and windows tall as a man, when I arrived, stood empty. I could have held it to my ear and heard the sea. Deborah away at rehearsal, David simply away (what else could I say just now?), out in the world somewhere. Cars past those windows followed headlights leading them like faithful horses towards the Barcaloungers, big TVs, barbeque grills and backyard swingsets that defined their riders' lives. Few surprises when these crews disembark.

I brewed coffee, heated milk in a long-handled pan that looked to have been strip-mined at some point for its copper, poured them together into a mug the size of a soup bowl. Rocker and floor, old friends, spoke to one another as I settled. From half-toppled stacks on the table alongside and tucked beneath, guided by who knows what instinct, specific hunger, chance, I fingered out Gustav Meyrink's *The Golem,* a book I'd had for years but never got around to.

The moonlight is falling on to the foot of my bed. It lies there like a tremendous stone, flat and gleaming.

As the shape of the full moon begins to dwindle, and its right side starts to wane—as age will treat a human face, leaving its trace of wrinkles first upon one hollowing cheek—my soul becomes a prey to vague unrest. It torments me.

At such times of night I cannot sleep; I cannot wake; in its half dreaming state my mind forms a curious compound of things it has seen, things it has read, things it has heard—streams, each with its own degree of clarity and color, that intermingle, and penetrate my thought.

There was moonlight now, like a blanket, a shawl, thrown across my lap, making me the very image of an old man at rest, idly musing. I recalled Lee Gardner writing to me of a friend's death, a writer he'd edited for years, and of the article by some self-styled expert briefly praising Lee's friend, then going on at length to complain how he'd been lured away from "legitimate" novels by the temptation of huge sums of money to be made in writing genre fiction. Huge sums of money? Lee had asked, incredulous, in his letter. Legitimate novels? And still more incredulously: Sour obituaries—is this what we all come down to?

Most of our lives come down to far less, of course.

Long ago I'd given up trying to keep count how many times my own had gone south, gone sour, gone dead still. I'd think I knew where I was headed, every station, every stop, two dollars for the box lunch that came aboard at Natchez or Jackson tucked in my shirt pocket, only to find myself waylaid to some unsuspected sidetrack, engine long gone, mournful call fading.

That was the shape my son's life took, too, whatever the explanation. Some errant braid in the genes, mother's madness encoded, encysted and passed down the line; chaos dropping (we'd expected another caller) on a swing from above. As though all his life David had been scaling this huge mountain of sand. Some days, some years, he'd manage to kick in footholds and stay in place, maybe even hoist himself up a yard or two. But the sand always gave way.

The phone, I realized, had been ringing for some time. As I stood, the manteau of moonlight fell away from my lap. I crossed to the hall table and picked up the receiver. Quiet enough itself, my "Yes?" tipped headfirst into silence.

Someone there at the other end, though.

After a moment I hung up. Almost at once the phone began ringing again. I ignored it. The ringing stopped, then restarted. Beating its jangly chest till I capitulated.

"Lew? Were you sleeping?" Deborah.

"Not really. You just call?"

"Started to. Then someone needed something—right away, of course."

"Don't they always? Makes you feel important, though. Needed. How many of us are given that?"

"You're saying this is a gift?"

"Hey, you have to unwrap it, it's a gift, right?"

"Hmmmm."

"Wow. A polyester necktie with violins on it! An ant-farm picture frame! An electric hot dog grill!"

"Hmmmm again. How'd your day go?"

"Not bad. Stuck its head out of the water some earlier than I'd have liked. And now the tail keeps wagging."

"T-a-i-l? Or t-a-l-e?"

"Either, I guess. Both."

"Think any more about your book—if it is a book?"

"Haven't had much chance to." I told her about

my visit to Don, what he was planning. Then about my expedition to the morgue with Santos.

"I'm sorry, Lew. Listen . . ."

Across the street, someone dressed all in gray, as though wearing tatters of the night itself, hove into view. He carried an old-fashioned red kerosene lantern, swinging it back and forth and shouting what well might have been (at this distance I saw only the motion of his lips) All aboard! Though he could as easily have been calling Bring out your dead, searching for an honest man, or just seeking warmth.

Surprising how we subtropical folk got used to the cold. Coming to take it so much for granted that we'd stopped remarking it. An adaptable lot. I stood now, blanketless, chill, watching the plume of my breath stream out, balance for a moment before me, fade.

"Rehearsal's going . . . well . . . oddly, I guess might be the best description. But good. We're onto something here, and reluctant to shut it down. I may not be home for a while."

"You get a chance to eat?" She'd gone directly from work to rehearsal, I knew, and rarely ate lunch. "I could bring you something."

"We ordered out. Soup, sandwiches, coffee, beer. Should be here any minute. We've all been hitting it pretty hard, and we were starving. Thought we'd take a break first, then tuck heads down and give a try to plowing on through, see where we get. Just a second, hang on." Someone had spoken to her, and she turned away briefly to answer. "Lew . . ."

"Still there?" I said after a moment.

"Yeah. Yeah, still here. Guess I will be for some time too, from the look of it. Here, I mean. You be okay?"

"Sure I will."

Enormous shadow accompanying him, the man came back along the sidewalk with his lantern.

"I was sitting outside the theater tonight waiting for everyone to show. Tired beyond belief, exhausted really, but at the same time excited, eager. There were these rings and loops around everything, like auras, street and sidewalks and the edges of buildings vibrating, trembling. I didn't know if that was because of the light or just because I was so tired. Dark was coming on fast, and I remembered your telling me how, when you were a child back in Arkansas, you'd sit in your backyard trying to watch it get dark. After a while you'd look around and realize it had gone several degrees darker but that you hadn't been able to see the change as it happened. We never do, do we?

"Sorry, Lew," she said. "I'm just fantastically, incredibly, unbelievably tired. When I'm this tired, my mind's all over. Nothing connects and everything seems to. Listen, don't wait up, okay? I'll see you in the morning."

"Have a good rehearsal."

I put the phone down with the sure sense that I was letting go of something far more than a conversation; with the sense, too, that there was little enough I could do to change this.

Or maybe it's just my storywriter's sense, all these years later, telling me that.

15

oy's been sick, Lester said. Took to his bed and won't be budged, over a week now. Never done that before. I'd gone across for coffee and doughnuts from the Circle K. Lester held his plastic cup on one bony knee, vinelike fingers wrapped around. We'd both wisely foregone the doughnuts after tasting them. Pigeons strutted happily among their dismembered remains.

Maybe I could go see him.

Don't know as how it would do any good. But if you could spare the time, the boy does seem to have taken to you, in his own way. Meaning only (I thought) that occasionally, in his own way, he acknowledged my existence.

We walked four, maybe five blocks. A square, Federal-looking house set almost flush with the sidewalk, columns thick as pecan trees on the shallow gallery out front, two stories, peach with darker trim, faux gable stuck atop like a stubby birthday candle. We went up wooden external stairs painted industrial gray through a wrought-iron gate, multiple locks and frosted-glass front door into the entryway. Folks are away, Lester said. Table inset with lime-green tile there, vase of yellow, hopeful flowers on it. Mail stacked alongside. Floor itself tile, darker green, light blue. Up more stairs then to the boy's room. Mattress in a corner, chair by the window. Cardboard box on its side, packed neatly with food: boxes of crackers, squares of cheese, cans of Vienna sausage, potted meat, bags of carrots, celery. Boy doesn't take much to beds, Lester explains, just plain will *not* sleep in one. Won't sit at table either, or eat like reg'lar folk—shaking his head.

But I understood. This food was the boy's own, forage, stockpile. He had no further need to go out into the world for it, no need to ask anything more of that world, anything at all, at least for a while. Here in his cave, on this pure, bare island, he'd become self-contained, self-sufficient, insular, hermetic, whole.

All man's problems, Pascal said, derive from the simple fact that he is unable to remain quietly alone in his room.

The boy, just as Lester reported, lay on the mattress. On his right side, knees drawn up, so that he faced me when I sank to the floor just inside the door. My own knees stuck up like a cricket's. I'd put my back to the wall and slid down it. God. I used to be able to do this, and it doesn't seem so long ago, with ease. Now garden tools dig at my joints and I fight for breath. Cramps announce themselves: arriving on track four.

The boy and I sat looking at one another. His eyes wide, unblinking. Does something, recognition, sympathy, identification, pass between us? Is there a message, is there feeling, even comprehension, in those eyes? How can I know? They're like stone artifacts left behind, the menhirs of Carnac, unreadable.

Then the boy worked his mouth a moment and made sounds.

What was that?

You got me, Lewis, Lester said from the doorway. Miracle, some might be inclined to say. Boy's never spoken before. No one thought he could. . . . Big uns?

Pigeons.

You're right. It could be.

What about them? I asked the boy. What about the pigeons? What are you trying to tell me?

His mouth worked silently for a time before producing again (at what unimaginable cost?) that same indecipherable sound.

Here I squatted at cave's mouth, a midwife attending language's birth, witnessing urgencies that over hundreds of years, a thousand, would shape themselves into human speech. Lester shifted feet beside me in the doorway. Downstairs the phone rang. On the third ring, the answering machine picked up. Again, momentarily, I became a child: comforting voices from other rooms, grown-ups out there doing drinks and dinner parties, extending the ever-elastic day while I lie tucked away safe and warm in nighttime's folds.

We waited, but the boy failed to speak again. When at last I stood, hauling myself up with one hand on whatever I could reach, wincing at pain and stiffness, his eyes didn't follow.

I could have said many things as Lester and I trudged together down the stairs. That the boy had identified somehow with the park's pigeons, taking their illness, their immobility—all he could understand of death?—for his own. That with the extreme posture of his stillness he'd found a way to speak, a way to express his grief. Instead I said that I was sorry and hoped the boy might soon get better. Lester thanked me for coming.

It was my day for casualty reports. Earlier I'd gone to see Alouette. She'd been up and about and doing well for some time, but two days ago that bearable pain along the incision became something more; she woke with a fever and with (her words) maggoty white pus oozing from the site. A two-hour wait and five-minute visit at her OB/GYN confirmed the obvious diagnosis of infection. So now she was supposed to be back on bed rest, pushing fluids, cleaning the incision regularly with peroxide, gobbling dollar-a-capsule Keflex. I found her sitting at the kitchen table, laptop propped awobble on stacked books and phone cradled to one ear, little LaVerne asleep alongside in what looked like a dishpan lined with towels bearing pictures of teakettles, iron skillets, yellow squash, carrots.

As usual, the backdoor stood open, screen unlatched.

"Don't blame me," Alouette said, looking up from computer and phone, when I stepped through. "She likes it there, it's the only place she'll go to sleep. I laugh at your sixty-dollar cradle! your tapes of mother's heartbeat!"

"You really shouldn't be sitting here with the door unlocked."

"So everyone says." Back to the phone. "Look, I don't mean to interrupt, but you're telling me Judge Haslep isn't in town? Even though he had a full docket today and has another scheduled tomorrow? Why am I supposed to believe this?"

She motioned me to sit.

"You'll get back to me? Gee, I sure hope so." Sweetest voice possible. "Within the hour? Before I start dialing up some other numbers here on my Rolodex, asking if *they* know what's going on?"

Thumbing the phone dead, she set it down.

"Every bit of your mother's charm."

"God, I hope so. Worked for her. Get you something?"

"I'm good. You?"

"Absolutely."

"I do have to say it doesn't look much like a bed in here. Which is where, according to my information, you're supposed to be?"

She shrugged. "Larson." Word and shrug alike conveying this comic sense of the burden she had to carry, alas. "So why is it he talks to you when he never talks to anyone else?"

"Must be the honest face. Maybe like any good tribesman he values my experience as an elder. Or at the other end of civilization, merely defers to my status as cult novelist."

"My God, you don't think he can *read*, do you?"

"Stranger things have happened."

"Besides, I thought you gave all that up."

"More like I was given up. Not that you'd be changing the subject. . . ."

A beat, as Deborah and her actors would say. "I feel fine, Lew. Little Verne's fine."

"That's good. We'd all like to keep it that way."

She pushed the phone to one side, a dinner plate she was done with. "I'm not going to get out of talking about this, am I?"

I shook my head.

She typed in several lines, hit the mouse, glanced at the screen and hit it again. Then in a gesture of capitulation raised her hands, fingers spread. Pushed back from the table.

"The messages began about the time I learned I was pregnant. Just a sentence or two at first, scrawled on postcards. I didn't think too much about them."

"Unsigned."

"Always. I'd wonder, but how far can you go with nothing to go on?"

"You didn't save them? Didn't take any notice of postmarks?"

"Why would I?"

"And these were what—standard post-office issue? Picture postcards?"

"Well . . . at first a lot of them were like those god-awful slick cards from souvenir shops. Antelopes with jackrabbit ears, talking cactus wearing sunglasses, 'Back to the grind soon' with the drawing of an office coffeepot, that sort of thing. The messages were just as generic. Wish you were here. Hope you're well. Missing you."

"Then at some point they changed?"

"So slowly as to go unremarked."

From time to time her mother's speech leapt to the surface in Alouette's, word choice, cadence, attitude. Fishhooks in the heart.

"After a while I began to have the feeling that the cards were getting selected rather than picked at random. A stunning photo of Alaska with 'It never gets fully dark here' written on the back, for instance. There's some deeper message there, I'm sure. *Was* sure. Though I had and have absolutely not the barest ghost of an idea what it might be."

"Nothing directly threatening."

"Nothing overt. Nor ever, really. More the feel of it all. This presence forever refusing to announce itself but always palpably *there*."

Catching a thought on the wing, she pushed back up to the computer to type it in. I remembered La-Verne telling me, You're never completely here, with me, when you're working, are you, Lew?

"Sounds like classic paranoia, doesn't it?" Alouette said.

"Exactly the response a stalker wants to elicit. . . . I've seen your GOK file, you know."

"I was wondering when you'd bring that up. *If* you'd bring it up."

"Everything about it—your taking pains to tuck it away, that it exists at all—suggests you must have taken the whole affair more seriously than you claim."

From within the dishpan on the floor alongside came the scuttling sound of small legs and arms. "Hungry again," Alouette said. Fishing little Verne out, she bared a breast and put the baby to it.

"I do have to wonder, though, Lew. How is it you manage to avoid seeing this as a violation of privacy? All those rights and principles you uphold so heartily—what, they just go by the way when it becomes personal? And you have no qualms about the dishonesties involved?"

"Of course I do."

She shifted the child against her chest. "Of course you do. I'm sorry, Lew. I know it's not that simple."

"What is?"

"And I do appreciate your taking time to look into this. Though it's probably nothing."

"Probably. But it's okay with you if I keep poking around, right?"

"Sure it is. But talk to me about it, all right?" The baby kept sliding down; with one arm under, Alouette kept shrugging her back up. "I need to give Deborah a call about getting you guys over here for dinner sometime soon, too. Been way too long. How's Don, by the way?"

"Doing good. Over the worst of it. Should be home in a day or two." I told her about Derick, about Don's latest notion. Then took leave of Alouette to wend my own way homeward—through the thickening hubbub, as Wordsworth has it. By the park to draw from its

well, from Lester and his young charge, whatever so-
lace I could, then over sidewalks heaving up like
sculpted waves above the roots of ancient trees, Spanish moss overhead, buildings sharecropped into ruin
all about. Everything and everyone I knew a casualty.
Some of war, but most of us casualties instead of sub-
tler things: ambition, expectation. Of sex, history, our
families; of what is within us or therein lacking. Eco-
nomic casualties, too. Washed away in the floods
pushing downhill from America's scripture of progress
and spilling out over the banks of the gospel according
to market economy, privilege and special interest, in-
undating us. Casualties of the system.

Almost home, I passed my favorite statue in all of
New Orleans, a Confederate officer astride his horse.
Time had not been good to him. His name on the
statue's base was unreadable beneath a century's
mildew, and though protected by the historical society, here he was stuck on a tiny plot of land between a
sandwich shop and low-end apartment house. Both
front legs of his horse were in the air, signifying that
he'd died in battle. One aloft would have meant he
died of wounds sustained in battle; all four aground,
that he'd died of natural causes. All our statues, all
our horses, should have both front legs in the air. Casualties everywhere.

It was, as I said, my day for casualty reports. I got
home, found a starving cat and a message to call
528-1433, took care of the first though perhaps not
(and never) to his satisfaction, dialed the second and
after two rings had an uptown, quiet-spoken Yes? at
the other end. Lew Griffin, I told her. Please hold.
Moments later, a heavy breather.

"Thank you for returning my call, Mr. Griffin. I
was not at all certain you would do so."

I waited.

"Perhaps apologies are in order? I had not intended to catch you unaware. I thought you would know to whom you were speaking. That Mrs. Molino had seen to that."

"I know."

"Ah. Good, then. It's been many years since we last spoke. A call much like this one, as I remember. I hope you've been well?"

Silence slalomed down the wires.

"I realize that you don't like me, Mr. Griffin. This is as it should be: I've given you no reason to. Nor do I require or particularly desire your approbation." His sentences fell into place, space and silence between, like bricks being set into a wall. "I do, however, ask that you hear me out now—if that much is possible?"

"Go ahead."

"Thank you. I am calling . . . Excuse me." He turned away from the phone. Four coughs rang out like distant rifle shots. Then he was back. "There is an individual I have need to locate. Purely a personal matter. In the past, I'm told, such searches were a specialty of yours. I wonder if perhaps you might consider, if there were some way I might persuade you to undertake, locating this individual for me."

"Your sources were correct when they said 'in the past,' Dr. Guidry. I don't do that work anymore."

"I see. . . . They told me that as well, of course. Nonetheless I felt it imperative to ask. In which case, perhaps you could recommend me someone else? Another . . . practitioner?"

I gave him Boudleaux's name, address, e-mail, phone and fax numbers.

"A moment. Let me . . . Yes, I have it. Thank you."

Silence in the wires again, that vacuum, that pull.

"I have become, I understand, a grandfather," he said at length. "Alouette and the child, they are both well?"

"They are."

"Very good. Then—" Again he turned away, into that chesty coughing. "Mr. Griffin, could you hold a moment, please?" the quiet, uptown voice asked. Moments later Guidry was back, apologizing. "Might you possibly prevail upon the girl to call me, Mr. Griffin? It would mean a great deal to me. I—"

This time he didn't come back, and after a moment the quiet voice said, "I'm afraid Dr. Guidry has become indisposed. He does appreciate your help, Mr. Griffin."

Voice still there at the other end, waiting.

"I'm not at all sure the doctor would want me to tell you this, Mr. Griffin. Actually, I'm fairly certain that he wouldn't. But nowadays, with no one else available to take these decisions, I've only my own counsel to fall back upon."

She paused.

"The thing is, Dr. Guidry is dying. An advanced cancer of the prostate, that he seems to have known about for some time yet, whatever his reasons, chose to leave both unremarked and untreated. I have no way of judging whether this might affect your response to his request. I did feel you should know."

"Thank you—Mrs. Molino, is it?"

"It is. Catherine. And Mr. Griffin?"

"Yes."

"It is I who answers the phone, on this line, always . . . should you happen to call again."

16

MORNING's minion. Dappled dawn-drawn falcon towing in its wake besides the new day, like a ragman's cart, this wagonload of old. Breath a white plume above, Deborah's pale body alongside. Both of them oddly insubstantial? Bellies of frost at the base of the window. Birds outside richly achitter as though seeking news of the tropics so soon and suddenly departed. Surely one of them's heard something.

Like a tired swimmer, I turned onto my side, skimming the surface of this day. Land behind, land ahead. Neither in sight.

So many in my life fallen, gone so quickly. My parents, LaVerne, Alouette's first child. The man I killed up by Baton Rouge as oil rigs wheezed beside us, flat birds' heads rocking and pecking on their tethers. Can that really have been almost forty years ago? Before long, before anyone notices, Raymond Carver wrote, I'll be gone from here, and was. Or Rilke in "Portrait of My Father As a Young Man." He sees the dreams in his father's eyes, the prehensile brow like his own, all the rest so contained and unknowable that, even as Rilke looks on, the image of his father begins fading into the background: O quickly disappearing photograph in my more slowly disappearing hand. My own photograph would look much the same. Soon enough we all fade from whatever records, whatever impressions, there are of us. Fade like Rilke's father into time itself, the gray batting forever at our backs. Might David one day, looking at a photograph of me, sense something of those same longings? I remembered the photo of my young parents sitting together, smiling and happy, on the hood of their Ford. A woman I did not recognize—where in the embittered, joyless mother I grew up alongside was this pretty young woman hiding?—and a man I knew but slightly better, a man who had faded into the background long before his time, at the very start of mine.

The birds' tropics would be back, of course. They had only to wait here, gossiping among themselves. But my mother's happiness, the happiness I saw in that photo, once fled never returned. Would David?

LaVerne was gone. Baby Boy McTell. Hosie Straughter. Harry, the man I killed up by Baton Rouge. Don's son. All of us, eventually. Before long, before anyone notices.

You're always quoting other people, Verne told me once. Anytime something important happens or some thought logjams in your head, there you are, hopping up like a schoolboy, pick me! pick me! with what Dante or Camus or Thingamabob said. You think anyone gives half a damn, Lew? And half the time, anyway, you're only using it to avoid digging in, avoid having to find out what *you* think. Or what you feel.

Deborah's arm came across my shoulder, pulling me up from the depths, back safely to land. (Did I struggle? Drowning men often do.) Spread of sunlight on every surface. Wall and curtain, bureau, night-stand, quilt, rib cage. Whole world become surfaces now: how long will they hold? I feel Deborah's breath on my neck as she pushes into me. Warm the whole of her length, she smells faintly of sweat. Blankets and history, even this morning light, weigh us down.

"You're awake," she said.

"Oh yeah. Courtesy of our friends the birds."

"Who won't have us missing a single moment of this exciting new day."

"Not to mention Bat, who's been in here at least twice already, demanding to know why his food's not been replenished."

"Or the pneumatic truck collecting curbside garbage." Grunting and sucking air through pursed lips, slamming hands against wall and headboard, she did a great take on bad brakes, tailgates, whirring pickup motors.

"Ah, civilization."

"Not just *Twelfth Night* and Faulkner, is it, Lew?"

"Or Ricki Lake."

"Point taken."

Then: "Got some good points there yourself."

"Hard little buggers, aren't they? Anytime I have my period I get horny—you know that, right?" Her free hand moved down, rested on my stomach. "Sleep okay?"

"Mostly. I had this dream that seemed to go on and on all night, though I'm sure it didn't. Couldn't have. We were getting ready for a trip, fitting things into the car. Two friends (in the dream I knew who they were, even if I'm clueless now) had these old coins with distinctive dates, dates that jumped out at you, nickels I think. They kept putting them down in front of us, wherever we were. We'd be drinking cof-fee, one of them would come along and slap down a nickel there between cups. Standing on queue at a movie premiere—you looked quite wonderful, by the way, wearing one of your crinkle skirts, low heels, a sleeveless sweater, long earrings—there they were again with the nickels."

I turned towards her. We made necessary adjustments, tugged at covers.

"Damn cold, isn't it?"

"Houses just aren't built for it."

"Neither are we."

We lay there quietly for a time.

"Play going okay?"

"Way better than I have any right to expect. Turned into something of a marvel last night, actually. Everyone felt it at the same time. Suddenly the play wasn't us: we were the play."

"That's good."

"It's what you work for. You never know if it's going to happen." Moments later she added: "Most of the time it doesn't."

Doors slammed shut and dogs barked outside. A car alarm racketed on. Cans and bottles rang together as a neighbor emptied trash. From open windows in a third-floor apartment across the street, Mahler fought his way up through strings and brass to a deafening crescendo.

"Time for us to put the nickel down, Lew?"

Whatever the nickel was.

17

OBVIOUSLY this man has come to and found himself onstage. He looks about him, off to the wings, out at the audience. Then back to the wings, where a prompter reads him a line. He repeats it. The stage crew comes on and begins carrying off parts of the set, a chair, a screen, a table, as he speaks, looking back and forth from prompter to audience. Then a second person steps out and begins speaking. Their stories, we soon realize, interweave. And now there's a third. . . .

Something familiar, too, in what they're saying.

I recognize lines from *Suddenly Last Summer* just as Deborah leans towards me to whisper: Ionesco. The crew reappears, lugging yet another character in its wake, and goes back offstage bearing further bits and pieces of the set, a bookcase, a teapot, leaving this new character behind. Like the first, he looks about, disoriented. Then lines of Sartre spring from his lips, not *The Flies,* I think, something a bit more obscure.

Molière, O'Neill, Ben Jonson and Vian soon follow.

Gradually we come to realize that these are characters left over, as it were, from other plays, secondary characters, supporting roles—all those to whom, in whose stage lives, nothing much happened.

Afterwards at a coffeehouse on Magazine, as I watched powdered sugar from beignets drift in a blizzard onto her dress and café au lait's breath struggle up from the cup, Deborah was quiet.

"I miss it, Lew."

"Theater, you mean."

"It's as though something's been torn from me. As though there's this huge vacant lot in the middle of my life, buildings all around."

"So plant a garden. Take back the lot."

"It can't be that easy, can it, Lew?"

And of course it wasn't. In the weeks following, Deborah began play after play, at length abandoning them all.

"It's gone," she said, weeping against me in the deep of night. "How do people live without passion, without that one bright blue light? How do they go on without something central in their life?"

We were agreed on the idiocy of good advice, that only a fool would give it, a greater fool accept it. That night, three in the morning with Deborah's body shuddering against me and wind padding predatorily about outside, was no different.

"That's what people do," I said. "They go on."

18

I WASN'T looking for him, you understand.

Long since an adult, he was equally capable of making his own choices and declining to make them; he'd never hedged at accepting the fallout from either. Nor could I plead to having had much impression or influence on his life, not having been around to offer understanding, a sympathetic ear, least of all an example. I knew something, myself, about not making choices.

So as I rummaged the city, touching down with beer-drinker fishermen at their ordained posts on the levee off Tchoupitoulas, benching myself to reminisce in a statue-guarded, pie-slice park on Magazine, prowling Decatur with its shoulder-narrow sidewalks and balconies like shrugs above, wading across river-wide Canal down Esplanade to the Faubourg Marigny and rising back up through the Quarter past Simple Suzies, Eds and Professor Bills, past lean-to missions with tureens of watery soup and hope, past the library and City Hall, Leidenheimer Bakery, wooden stoops and swayback cement stairways, shipwreck islands of storm-tossed furniture, cable spools and milk crates on the neutral ground, I wasn't looking for my son.

For something within myself, rather. At some level that's what all our searches are about, of course.

"Can't help you much, Lew," his mother said that morning when I called. "Far as I knew, everything was going well. Last heard from him—I'd have to check to be sure—four, five weeks back? One of those trademark postcards of his, where the message starts off in regular script and becomes ever more crabbed, final sentences squeezed in sideways at the margins or asterisked in between lines."

"No sense of what was going on in his life?"

"You're kidding, right? You know what those cards are like. Sometimes he'd touch down, sure. Bring up some play or movie or concert he'd seen, string together bits of overheard conversation, remark that both of you'd taken to hanging around the house too much. Mostly, though, he just wrote about what he saw at his job. People he got to know there, *their* stories, where they lived, how. Hang on, I've got to pull something out of the oven." Two, three minutes later she was back. "Been a long time since we've talked, Lew."

"True enough."

"No reason for that, you know. You have my address, you could write from time to time, even do something outrageous like send the occasional Christmas or birthday card. Scrawl a satirical line or two in there if it made you feel better, whatever space's left. A quote, maybe, something appropriately snarly. Swift, Laurence Sterne, Thomas Bernhard, like that. It's always Serious Friday somewhere."

Serious Fridays had begun as a joke when David and his friends were students, all of them casually bohemian. No television, parties, dumb movies or other mindless escapism allowed on Fridays, the screed read. Exalted conversation only. High-end jug wine. Smelly, mysterious cheese. Books tucked underarm, coolly they'd stroll towards bars and ethnic restaurants, skirling intellectual happy hours like bullfighter's capes about them out there in a hot world.

"I hadn't imagined there was any way you'd want to hear from me, Jane. Christmas, Serious Friday, or otherwise."

"Well—" She turned away. "Hey! You see me, right? One standing here by the kitchen counter? knives all around? Don't want to spend the rest of your life reaching for things with two blunt forearms, hobbling about on ankles, right? Get away from my bread!" Back to me then. "All that was a long time ago, Lew. We were young together. Shared the very beginnings of our lives. We won't ever have that with anyone else, will we? It binds us."

"Those beginnings lasted, what, about ten minutes?"

"And the marriage not much longer—I know." Silence fell like Joyce's snow along hundreds of miles of wires, up past bayou and swampland, Whiskey Bay, Grosse Tête, through stands of ancient cypress, on into wildest America. "Nothing turns out the way we think it will, Lew. We don't know much else, but we know that. And if life's about anything, it's about all those twists and twinings and sudden turns and trapdoors, about learning to get lost gracefully."

I said I'd be in touch and, fortified with a troop-sized cup of coffee and a bagel I could have used help from that same troop in chewing, entrained for my sentimental journey. Steamed out of port past K&Bs and Circle Ks, chewed-up, century-old homes, abandoned storefronts sheathed in plywood so pitted and weather-worn that it resembled bark. Tchoupitoulas, Prytania, St. Charles, Jackson, Decatur. Streetcars teeming with

tourists, black maids headed home with cash pay rolled
and tucked into garters and waistbands after the day's
work uptown, children gone hunchback from knapsacks of schoolbooks and video games. Mule-drawn
carts stood at idle alongside Jackson Square; limos
skimmed the city's surface like sharks; battered delivery
trucks, mopeds and bicycles hauling makeshift carts
rose and sank in random patterns. Cats beside buildings crouched over invisible meals and shot glances
past shoulders as I drew abreast. Children's faces
turned up from tricycles, peered out from latticed re-
cesses beneath porches. By one apartment house,
garbage bags sat piled in a black honeycomb, aloud
with the hundreds of flies buzzing inside them.

In a bar on St. Philip I came across Doo-Wop
holding forth to a busload of bulky, fair, rather square-
faced tourists, Finns possibly. Half a dozen drinks sat
aligned on the table before him. A Sony recorder, like
Doo-Wop hard at work, ground away there too. The
tourists were ordering round after round, eating with
greasy fingers from baskets of what purported to be
alligator tails and smiling broadly at one another, the
barmaid, Doo-Wop, the jukebox, signs on the walls
advertising beer, the walls themselves.

"Gitcha sump'n?" the barmaid asked. She was
twenty maybe. Looked well on the way to piercing
everything possible. We all need short-term, long-
term goals.

"Draft."

"On tap we got—" Gold stud in her tongue flash-
ing into view like a Christmas tree ornament hidden
away.

"Whatever," I said. "All pretty much the same,
isn't it?"

"I guess."

"These people have any idea what's going on?"

She shrugged. "How you gonna know?"

She brought me a glass of something that the other beers probably beat up every day on its way home from school. Felt kind of sorry for the poor thing, actually. I'd taken a seat at bar's end in half darkness and now, price of the ticket paid, was able to focus on Doo-Wop's performance.

"This was back in the golden days, you understand, no reason back then to doubt any of it. Did what we did so other Americans could get on with their lives. Eternal vigilance and all that. Hell, we were saving the free world single-handedly. You-all understand free world, right? Single-handedly?

"Good.

"Twice a day, then, flying at treetop level to stay just below radar, I'd make my way towards Cambodia. I'd climb in the cockpit with floppy mailbags and come back with them packed full. Most days I flew a modified—Captain!"

Doo-Wop had caught sight of me. He stood, sole of one shoe flapping forward of the hemp twine he'd secured it with. A bright yellow sportcoat hung heavy as stage curtains from his shoulders. Below, as though under its protection, an aqua shirt, bottle-green tie, chocolate trousers. He'd come up out of his chair and away from the table set with drinks to shake hands. Don't think I'd ever seen him do that before. I felt as though history itself had gone on pause.

"Been a long time, Captain."

"It has."

"You still turning out them books?"

I nodded. "Just like you're still turning out looking *good.*"

He glanced down at what he was wearing. God knows what he saw, what he thought.

"New Bargain Town opened up just last week, up on Oak. Where that shoe store used to be? Rack after rack of fine product ripe for the picking. Great coun-

try, this." He smiled out on the prospect of his
tourists, waved an apologetic hand. "Be done here
shortly, Captain," he said. Point of honor: he had to
repay with stories the drinks advanced him. "You be
able to stick around?"

I said I would and settled in. Doo-Wop returned to
his table, where he became by turns a park ranger at
Yellowstone, a businessman from "one of those mid-
western states starting with *I* where all the suburbs
have the same name," a bus driver from Montgomery
convinced he knew what had happened to those kids
and had seen the man responsible, an accordionist
named Jimmy who for over thirty years played happy
hour (never missed a day) at King's Inn in Memphis,
famous for his stylings of "Heartbreak Hotel," Jimmy
Reed songs and various Abba hits, and a retiree to
Phoenix who'd worked graveyard shift as security guard
for a Third Street transplant center until the night,
bored out of his mind, he'd added *Drive-Through Window* complete with arrow to the sign out front.

All of them, people Doo-Wop had crossed paths
with here in New Orleans. He'd pick up their stories
like shells off a beach. Sometimes in the drudge of afternoons I found myself watching all those TV shows
suddenly become so popular these last few years,
weekly movies "based on a real story," *Cops,* Ricki and
the rest, and I'd think: Doo-Wop had it down years
ago, long before any of them. Rumplestiltskinning the
straw and dross of the real to fool's gold.

He sat down beside me. "Well, *that's* done."

"Hard work."

"Not too many'd know that," he said after a moment.

The barmaid appeared tableside. Since I'd last
seen her she'd had a couple more piercings, I was sure
of it. "What would you like?" I asked Doo-Wop.

"What're you having?"

"Generic beer."

"Two of your best generics, Mandy," he said.

She smiled, adjusted a few rings and studs, and went off to bring the beers as I asked Doo-Wop if he'd heard about some guy or guys who were killing pigeons. I'd hung out by the park a couple of times, talked to people around the neighborhood, but hadn't come up with anything.

"Nope, but I'll keep an ear open. Look what I still got," Doo-Wop said, pulling one of my old business cards out of his wallet. I must have given it to him thirty years ago at least, about the time he got that wallet from the look of it, and he'd been carrying it ever since, the way some folks squirrel away newspaper clippings, till it was all but unreadable.

No continuity in our lives, huh?

I took the card from him, amazed, for a closer look. *Le*—though that *e* could as easily be an *o*. And *Griffin* could have been almost anything: Grief, Gripping, Garage, Cartage, Goring. Below, *Investigations* remained mostly readable, though the *v* had migrated—hoping to start up a word of its own, perhaps.

I had a sudden vision, one it was probably best not to dwell on, of Doo-Wop sitting behind the barricades of a beer and peanuts telling stories from his years as a local detective.

Mandy brought our beers. Definitely generic. Doo-Wop drank half his down in a single generic swallow.

"You used to teach, right, Captain?"

I nodded. Another previous life. How many had I had? Feeling a certain sympathy for that used-up business card.

"You know anything about this film department up to Loyola?"

"Other than the fact that there is one, not much." A year or two back, I'd attended a festival of student work and had dim memories of short films about a classics professor who lived in a trashcan out behind Antoine's, a giant panda lobbying for the NRA, an insect zoo, complete with tiny cages, kept in someone's dorm room.

We sipped our beers.

"Boy comes up to me over to Freret, the Come On In. You know it?"

No.

"Three people be in there and one of them goes to stand up, someone's gotta back out the door."

There used to be many such places scattered about the city. Bars in ground-level converted garages below apartments, one-room restaurants run out of family homes—like the Williams family snoball business that's made a fortune dealing shaved ice and flavors out the back of a garage without so much as a sign for three or four decades.

"But I go by most every day, 'cause you never know. Meet up with good folk there sometimes. So I'm sitting having me a beer talking to a dogcatcher works out by Gentilly and this boy comes in. He's wearing sunglasses and looking around in there trying to see and it's like he's forgot about them, thinking why the fuck's it so dark in here, and of course it *is* dark in here, but not *that* dark, you damn fool, I'm thinking. As who wouldn't. And he does look peculiar. White boy, mind you, but he's got these braid things sticking out ever' which way that look like they don't get washed 'cept when it rains and he's standing out in it, he's got on these shorts that the crotch of them's down around his ankles and you could pack three or four good legs in there. And this goddam backpack, bright orange with, I don't know, some kind of animal or something on there with a lot of teeth, grinning."

Mandy came back jingling, swinging and adjusting. Four more of the same, Doo-Wop said, we goan be here a spell.

"So," Doo-Wop went on once our beers arrived, "boy swings off that backpack and says, Doo-Wop, I presume? That grin and all those teeth are down by my ankles now. Can we talk, man?

"What're you gonna do?"

With no discernible cue, the tourists had formed a precise line just inside the door. Now the door sprang open, and they filed out bearing shoulder bags, fanny packs stuffed like Thanksgiving turkeys, souvenir glasses, six-packs of pralines, cheaply printed menus abounding in typos, greasy alligator tails wrapped in napkins.

"He's heard about me, this boy says. Says me and my stories are a local legend and that that's what New Orleans is, its history, all the stories. He's making a movie about the city and wants me to be a part of it. Been looking for me for a while now, he says. Wants me to be a kind of interlocutor, that's the word he used, have me talk some 'bout the rest, then they'd come on."

Doo-Wop drained off his first beer and picked up the second. "What you think?"

"Beats me."

"Me too. And it just beats all, don't it, the whole thing. But the more I think on it, the more I'm inclined to."

I raised my glass, my first, and still mostly full, to toast him. Three more squatted there by it. "Then maybe you should."

"Yeah, maybe. Probly. Why th'hell not. But hey, for now I gotta go, right?" He chugged his third beer and, hand pausing over the table as over a chessboard, pushed the last into line with my own. "Have to take care of business like always, don't I?"

I walked with him to the door. Outside, he pulled a bike from beneath the eaves. It was of the new generation, gears and toggles everywhere, high-tech tires.

He unlocked it, threw a leg across, crotch-walked it into sunlight.

"Something new?"

"You bet. Resplendent, ain't it?"

It was.

"Resplendent." He nodded, then shook, his head. "Just cain't get around like I used to. Boy wants to make that film, he up and gave it to me. Said why not, he don't never use it no more. *Someone* ought to get the benefit of it, boy said. Don't mind telling you it's been a blessing. Now I can *really* cover ground." This from a man who regularly, every day for well over forty years, had covered most of the city on foot.

"That's good. You take care, now."

"'Spect I will. Mostly have. You too, Captain. Don't let them beers back in there go wastin' neither." Halfway to launch, listing starboard on the seat, left leg cocked, Doo-Wop paused. "Word of advice?"

"Always."

"Boy asking after you as well. Had some stories he's heard, old ones for the most part, near as I can say. He don't tell them too good either, mind you. I thought you'd be wanting to know."

"Appreciate it, my friend."

"Welcome." And Doo-Wop went sailing off to whatever port came next.

That night I sat out in the slave quarters reading David's message again. I'd left on lights in the house and kept looking across, half-expecting heads and bodies to appear, as in previous, happier days, in that blazingly white kitchen.

I have no idea when you might find this—tonight, tomorrow, next week. I don't even know, really, how to begin it.

I read David's message over and over, slowly, leaving space around each word for it to expand, working

sememes and syllables like bread dough. At one point
I looked up to find Deborah's face there in the window over the sink, across the courtyard. She was
drinking a glass of water from the tap, and after she
put it down she waved, face tilting like a bird's to ask
should she come out. I shook my head. She blew a
kiss and laid head obliquely on joined hands: moving
towards sleep.

We always have to understand, don't we?

Life's not a particularly good editor, but it can
prove a quarrelsome one. David had careted in his
message among notes I'd been sketching for a novel.
There it was, rude actuality, thrusting up like a ragged
tree stump from my own pale version of the same. I
thought of David's postcards and how the texts of our
lives seem always overwritten, events scribbled in between lines, corrections tacked on at the end or written in at a slant.

Life for each man (this from Eugene O'Neill) is a
solitary cell whose walls are mirrors. Looking out, we
think we see someone signaling, a warning, a wave, a
plea. But it's only our trapped selves measuring with
hands the limits of their world.

From long habit, music forever asimmer on back
burners as I worked, I'd turned on the radio when I
settled in out here. Classic jazz had given way to a
talk show on which prizefighter Eldon Truman was
being interviewed, and I came skittering to a stop on
its surface.

Scooped from the street following a series of central Baltimore burglaries, Truman went on to spend
some twenty-six years in America's worst prisons. Two,
three minutes into the interview, Truman, a biography
of whom had just been published, took exception to
the host's use of the word *commune* and went on taking exception. Taking exception was a way of life, a

creed, for him. Just as in prison (he recounted) he'd refused to follow the white man's rules. Refused upon induction to divest himself of civilian clothing, of rings and necklaces, refused to have his hair cut. "They had to put me where the others couldn't see me, finally. Had to get me out of sight. Out of sight and mind, you see." Solitary. Out of sight there, he'd spent a dozen years reading law books obsessively, then (out of mind, many said) turned just as obsessively to metaphysics. Castaneda. Ouspensky. Husserl.

Phone calls came in from Al and Ian in Keokuk, Iowa, Sharon in Sharon Center, Georgia, Cheryl in Highland Park, Illinois, George from Irving, Texas, Roberto (call me Rick) out in Tucson, Arizona. They never tell us the truth, one caller said, never. Whatever they do tell you, just turn it over. Mr. Truman's right. Another said: Up here in the heart of the heart of the land, we've built us a model community. Grow our own food, bake our own bread. Simon called in to say there was so much wrong in the world, so much pain, and ended with a favorite quote, from Brecht: What times are these when a poem about trees is almost a crime because it contains silence against so many outrages? Bret from Milwaukee: The disparities just keep unfolding. Ever since Reagan, Bush, that sorry lot, water rising, a flood. Executives now pull down three hundred and twenty-six times the average worker's salary. How in God's name did this come about? And why do we let it go on?

I keyed in Select All and sat for a moment with my finger over Delete, then hit it. Notes for a novel that might have been, and David's message, washed away. Enough stray words in the world already.

"Somewhere, among the wastes of the world, is the key that will bring us back, restore us to our Earth and to our freedom," Pynchon wrote in *Gravity's*

Rainbow. That's where David was now, I hoped—out there in the wastes of the world where the keys are kept. And there in the dark (for now I'd shut off radio, computer and lights to welcome it) I bent my head into the vast silence that is our lives, and listened.

19

LEW. Do you hear me? Lew?"
I drifted up slowly, all the time in the world.
World up there waiting for me. Patient as grand-father's hand when we'd walk down by the river. I was four, maybe five, and he'd come up alongside the house, up the hill, hobbling, to fetch me. As a young man Grandfather had broken his leg. With no doctors around, his father built a box, a small tailored coffin, around it. He was a carpenter, this was what he knew. The leg healed, but forever afterward Grandfather listed to port and starboard with each step. As Grand-father came he'd be reciting some poem he'd learned back in school forty or more years ago. More like ninety, now, I guess. Longfellow, Whittier, William Cullen Bryant. The whole of "Thanatopsis" or "Snow-bound," Booth led boldly with his big bass drum. Not just reciting the poem, but declaiming it as had been the fashion in his youth, an auditory equivalent of Palmer penmanship. Lines, stanzas, rhymes spun and

leapt like dancers, like high divers, from his tongue, providing my earliest intimation that words might do more than simply express needs or convey information: that they could transform the world, recast it. Down we'd go then by the river, this hobbling old man and upreaching, diminutive me, past tar paper shacks and along the levee as barges lugged their tedious way upriver towards Memphis or down to Vicksburg and New Orleans, barrel-like pipes running out above and across (carrying what? I never knew), cement slabs piling up crisscross by the hundreds as trucks ran over legs and wood risers collapsed, burying workers paid $3.50 a day, at the slab field just south, the sandbar at river's center growing ever wider through the years. We'd bob and weave along the levee, through cement floodgates thick as tree trunks at the bottom end of Cherry Street behind the abandoned train station and just off Niggertown (where, at the Blue Moon Café, age ten or twelve, I saw my first live blues musicians—Sonny Boy Williamson and Robert Lockwood, I later discovered), and stop off for watery fountain Cokes in the alleyway behind Habib's. Habib's was run by one of two Jewish families in the town. Aside from the restaurant, they kept to themselves.

"Lew?"

No telling how much food went out that backdoor and down that alley year after year to those who might otherwise have gone without, itinerant farmworkers, folks in town hoping for positions at the tire and chemical plants, whole families trucked up en masse from Mexico to pick cotton, bluesmen in town playing jukes and streetcorners, local blacks, poor whites. All the lost tribes.

"Lew. Damn it, answer me!"

No longer was I drifting. Now I'd begun struggling my way upwards. Age ten or twelve, about the same time I came upon Sonny Boy and Robert Junior at the

Blue Moon, I saw *Houdini* at the Malco halfway up Cherry, from the balcony cordoned off, weekends only, 25 cents, for blacks. Wrapped in chains and shut away in a trunk, Tony Curtis got thrown into freezing water. He rose, manacles and trunks left behind, only to encounter a sky of ice.

But now the ice gives way and I'm moving up again, ever closer. Deborah's face swims into focus there above me. Lovely as always.

Years ago, after I found Alouette and her child, both desperately ill, in a hospital up in Mississippi, she told me what it was like to be so sundered from life. "Suddenly I broke free. Really free. I was floating. Nothing could touch me, nothing could hold me down. I remember thinking: How wonderful this is, I don't even have to breathe now."

But of course I did. Had to breathe and had to do it now, here, as I struggled upward, light digging into my eyes like fists. Where am I? What shore have I washed up on?

Now, I found, had become *then.* Another hole in my life.

"Hey, woman."

Halfway between sleep and waking, my mind takes up familiar things, turns them over, around. I stand in a tenement house watching figures move in the frame of windows opposite. It's hot and their windows, like mine, are open. I see their lips moving, hear the sound of their voices but can't make out what they're saying. Trying, I lean closer, out my window, and in that moment feel my balance giving way.

"Lew. You're back."

"I guess."

"We've been worried."

When I didn't respond (I was working on it, but words proved slow to shape themselves around my intentions), she went on. "Don, Rick Garces, Alouette. We've been taking turns. Larson even took a couple of shifts off to spell us, turned things over to his foreman. You've been out almost five days."

"Damn."

She told me the date.

"I don't remember a thing."

"You've had a stroke, Lew. A light one."

"Damn."

"Yeah. Damn."

"Light one," a voice says above me. Not Deborah's this time. Have another five days passed, or just moments? I've no way of knowing. No landmarks here, nothing to grab hold of. "You're lucky, Mr. Griffin." *In here* becoming *out there* in a flood, I open my eyes. Not Deborah's face either, unless she's grown a soul patch, pierced an ear. On the trade wind of his breath I smell coffee, raw sugar, milk that's just turned or is about to. "The world's been kind enough to send you a message. A warning. You're going to be okay. A month, six weeks from now, it'll be like nothing's happened. But next time . . ." Sincere face and brown eyes hover there over me. He's what, mid-twenties? Sees so much of life every day, been through so little of it himself.

More white space then, as the world again shut itself down. The doctor's face stayed up there a while, lips moving. Then it changed: grew larger, misshapen, grotesque; broke into parts and rolled away—as though in slow motion a stone had shattered a waterborne image.

When next the world washed back, Don and Jeeter were there at water's edge, talking. Don held a pint-size plastic cup of coffee in one hand. Every few mo-

ments he'd gesture with that hand to emphasize something he was saying, then catch himself just before
coffee sloshed over the top.

"Thing you have to look at," Don was saying, "is
how's it gonna travel? Sure it looks good right now,
but what about four years from now, or ten? Horse-
shoeing probably looked good, too, sixty or seventy
years ago."

"I hear you." Jeeter grinned. "Whatchu think 'bout
shepherding?"

"Don't mind me," I told them.

"All right," Jeeter said.

"Derick's trying to decide what he wants to be
when he grows up."

"So how you doin', Mr. Griffin?"

"I've been better."

"Worse, too," Don said.

"Can't argue with that."

"You be needing anything?"

I told the boy no.

"Be okay we talk a spell, then?"

"Sure."

"Lew may not feel like—" Don started, but I
waved him mute.

Jeeter pulled a molded plastic chair lost somewhere on the road between purple and blue, one size
fits none, up to the bed. When he sat, his knees came
almost level with his ears.

"Don's took me down to the library, got me a library
card. Lady with sequins on her glasses tells me I can
take home six books. Gotta be a million or so in there
at least, and I'm walking around wondering how'm I
gonna pick six books out of all those. And what about?
So I'm giving thought to all this stuff I've wondered
about, Joan of Arc, karate, old cars, the Vietnam War
my old man never got over, this Langston Hughes person I've heard of, and suddenly I remember how Don

told me *you* wrote some books. I go back to the lady with the sequins on her glasses and ask can she help me. Sure enough, she brings me this little stack of books. They're pretty beat up, so I guess I'm not the only one's looked into them, you know? I took the top six home—two of them were the same, but I didn't know that—and I read them all that weekend."

I glanced over at Don, still by the window. He nodded.

"Monday morning, I was there waiting when the library opened. The lady with sequins on her glasses had the day off. Young woman in a crinkly brown dress and sandals helped me that time. Her skin was white as rice, I remember. Kind of lumpy like it, too. She brought me another stack of books, some of them different, some the same. I went ahead and read them all."

"You have a new fan, Lew," Don said.

"I didn't know books could be like that, Mr. Griffin. None of the ones I'd ever saw before were."

"Thank you, Jeeter."

"Call me Derick."

"Derick, then. Thanks. I don't think I've ever had a finer review."

"He means it, Lew."

"So do I."

"I just keep reading those books over and over, Mr. Griffin, gotta been through some of them them five, six times by now. *Skull Meat, The Old Man, Mole.* You're writing about what I lived all my life, streets I grew up in, people I know. All of it right there. Something else going on there, too. Something I don't understand. I don't give up, I keep reading. But I just can't quite get hold of it." He grinned. "Sometimes I *almos'* do."

"Yeah. Sometimes I almost do, too."

✦

Dead still this morning. So still and bright with sun that you don't notice how cold it is until you move. Then the cold's after you with blades and saws. Deborah and I have talked all night. Now I ask her what day it is.

"Sunday."

Now that she'd told me, I heard bells from the Baptist church down the street. It had taken me days to figure out what was odd about the sound: the bells were electronic, starting up right on pitch and ending with no aftertones, volume at a level the whole time.

"And the date?"

It had become important to me, virtually an obsession, to know these things. Just as hour upon hour I found myself watching the clock. Hands that knocked knocked knocked without entering.

"Diversion, Lew," Deborah had told me, "misdirection. So you don't have to face the darker time ticking away inside you." Cold wasn't the only thing cutting to the bone these days.

Blearily I looked down at people huddled in the bus stop across the street four floors below. They wore whatever coats they had, and most held cups of coffee. Steam leaked like breath from their cups and from grease-stained bags of food. Cold waited till people stood or changed position on the bench, then pounced. Eye turned upwards and mouths writhed in pain.

"Brought some things to help get you through all this," Deborah had said, dipping into her backpack. I thought of *Madame Butterfly* ("I've brought a few things") as she held up a finger: "Some favorites." Montaigne's essays, *L'Écume des jours*. A second finger: "Also these." Tapes of cultural programs and game shows like *My Word* a friend dubbed off the BBC. Third finger, with dramatic pause: "And me, of course. . . ."

So we'd spent the night talking. About how rehearsals were going, latest reports from doctors, official confirmation that this was the coldest winter in a quarter century, when I was likely to get sprung.

"On that subject, I have a message for you from Don. He says if you try to walk out of here the way you usually do, he'll personally come after you, rope and hog-tie you, and bring you back."

I whistled a bar or so from Copland's *Rodeo*.

"He's serious, Lew. *This* is serious. You scared us." She was stacking books and tapes neatly on the bedside table. "Rick Garces wants me to tell you to hurry up and get well because he's got a new recipe he can't talk anyone else into trying. Sea insects. 'You know how picky them white boys is 'bout their food,' he says, ''specially the straight ones.' Dean Treadwell called from the school to see how you were and asked that I give you his best. The *Washington Post* said—I knew you had a piece due and gave them a call, hope you don't mind—not to worry about the Fearing review, they'd wait. And your agent says call her when you get a chance. There's a new publishing house in Scotland, run by a bunch of kids, Vicky says, but they seem to know what they're doing, that wants to talk to you about reissuing your books."

"Nothing from David?"

She shook her head. "I'm sorry, Lew."

A bus pulled up below and all climbed aboard. I had to wonder if any of them even cared where the bus was headed. It was warm at least, and you could stay aboard indeterminately. The bus pulled away, leaving bus stop and street alike empty, windswept, barren. As though the whole world itself had emptied. No one left alive.

"You going to be okay?"

I nodded. A nurse's head tilted in around the door. Red hair, full lips. "Mr. Griffin?" Then she came on in. Eyes green and alive, forever in motion, unbecomingly wide hips somehow still sexy, tattoo of barbed wire on one upper arm. "Physical therapy called, asked me to let you know they're on their way." Her name tag hung from a lanyard of multicolored beads, swaying as she walked: Erin. "Need anything before? Pain meds, new designer gown, box lunch?"

"Still no word, I take it, on my pardon from the governor?"

Sad face. "Sorry."

"Just as well. I absolve you all, you know."

"Of course you do."

When she was gone, Deborah came and lay beside me on the bed. My right hand cradled her stomach, my left embraced her. "We've had good times, Lew. Lots of them." Her hair was streaked with gray, strands of it. When had those shown up? Memory was so unreliable, such a liar. So self-serving. Only thing it did well was break your heart.

Down in the street a lowrider passed with speakers blaring so loudly that it set off alarms in parked cars as it passed. We lay there listening to them go off, one after another, as it cruised along.

20

I T ALWAYS escalates, Lew. You know that."

"She didn't want to bother me with it. Wanted to wait till I was out of the hospital at least, she said. I'm not sure she would have brought it up at all, if Larson hadn't pushed."

"So *he*'s concerned."

"Larson's the one who told me about it in the first place. Couldn't have been easy for him, either. He and Alouette have a strong relationship, if not one we'd think of as ordinary. They have their own, quite independent lives. Distinct personalities. But they're solidly together and respect one another's opinions, beliefs, decisions. Seems to be plenty of space left in the relationship for that."

"You're saying he saw coming to you with this as a violation."

I nodded.

Don stood, flexing back and shoulder muscles. He rolled his head forward and back, shoulder to shoulder. "Used to be I could sit for more than five minutes without everything stiffening up, you know?"

I knew.

"I don't keep moving, body's not the only thing's gonna stiffen up," Don went on. "So in past weeks there've been more of these messages."

"More of them, and closer together."

He glanced again at the one in his hand.

"Look, it's not like there's anything else I have to do, Lew. I can sit at home and spend my mornings worrying what's for lunch, or I can get up off my butt and onto this. Still have favors I can call in. Forensics, for a start. I'll have them take a look at this." He held up the note. "And the file from her computer at work. You got any problem with my talking to Alouette, asking her about it?"

"Not if she doesn't."

We were silent then. I've been blessed with good friends.

"Where are you?" Don said finally.

"I was remembering the first time I saw you, slumped against a wall downtown with blood pooling under you and garlic on your breath." The day he'd saved my life. "Then, later, how you showed up at my place with this yellow piece-of-shit BanLon shirt on. I mean, just how fucking white can you get?"

Don shrugged.

We'd been friends so long, been through so much together, that looking at him was a lot like looking in the mirror. And just as somewhere in your mind you stay twenty years old forever and are always slightly surprised when this old guy's head pops up in there, I was never quite prepared to see my friend looking so tired and worn down.

"You miss him, Don?"

Something we'd rarely spoken of since it happened. We found him, half afloat, half submerged, in the bathtub, plastic bag secured about his head.

"Every day of my life. I just keep thinking, if only I'd had the chance to get to know him better. If I'd *made* the chance, found it somehow."

"You did what you could."

"I don't know. . . . I know what he was, Lew. Like I told you then, it just doesn't seem to make much difference."

"He was right about one thing: Everything's water if you look long enough."

Don nodded. "From his note."

"Maybe it doesn't matter how much time you have. Maybe you're still left with all these piles of unfinished business."

Don sank back into his chair. "When did everything turn to past tense for us, Lew? You notice that happening?"

I shook my head.

He picked up the paper again. "You know what this is from?"

> If I have now made up my mind to write it is only in order to reveal myself to my shadow, that shadow which at this moment is stretched across the wall in the attitude of one devouring with insatiable appetite each word I write. It is for his sake that I wish to make the attempt. Who knows? We may perhaps come to know each other better.

"A Persian novel, *The Blind Owl*."

"Which of course you'd read."

"Not a clue. But it took Rick about two minutes flat to track it down on the Internet."

"And what is this? Drawn on?"

"Looks like someone did it on a computer, ran the typeface up to the point of blurring when he printed it out on an old dot matrix printer—not a well-maintained one, at that—then photocopied the printout. That's Rick's guess, anyhow."

"Why go to all that trouble?"

I shrugged. "Why send it in the first place? Maybe he thought he was covering his tracks somehow, maybe he sent copies to world leaders, stuck them under windshield wipers at the nearest mall. Who the hell knows? We think he may have been trying to make it look like an engraving."

"Okay. There's anything here useful, the lab'll find it." He held the paper up close. "That flytrack at the bottom some kind of signature?"

"I'm pretty sure it says William Blake."

"Tiger, tiger guy?"

I nodded. "Poetry was kind of a sideline for him, though. By trade he was an engraver. In his spare time he talked to angels."

21

Home I went, then, in due time, limping and scuttling. There on my island, I sat watching lives go on. Rain had come on like the fury it was, slamming away at houses and cars, lifting lawn appliances to abandon them half a block down and two across, slapping pedestrians to the ground. And everywhere the cold, attacking as much from within as without.

Between two roaring worlds where they swirl, I.

Yes, Mr. Joyce.

Meanwhile, the good ship Rick Garces came calling at my island. Never a lack of friends or good food when Rick's involved. This time, it was simple fare: polenta with wild mushroom sauce. Then he compensated with a salad of endive, baby green spinach, a handful of what looked like purple weeds, and slivers and bits of jicama, sweet cactus, sour German pickle. The mix of people, predictably, was as offbeat as the salad.

A couple of gay activists from NO AIDS arrived first, a longtime pair oddly enough, given that one (in vintage Capri pants and chambray shirt) was male, the other (wearing Fifties sharkskin suit and saddle-back shoes) female. All night long they stood side by side, a preponderance of sentences beginning "Eddie [or, conversely, Edie] and I . . ."

Next came a lawyer "down from Tulane, *way* down," working as he did exclusively pro bono cases. He sported the uniform of old New Orleans money, gray-and-white seersucker suit, starched shirt, bow tie. Luckily, he said, he'd been relieved of the burden of making a living and so was able to practice a purer form of law. And what better use (smiling) to which to put his family's ill-got money?

In fairly rapid succession, then:

A reporter in blue blazer and torn jeans from the *Times-Picayune*. (Hosie Straughter? Hell yes, I knew him!)

An emergency-room doctor whose color and fixed expression put one in mind of a Halloween pumpkin. In her wake trailed a retired FBI husband who, with half a bottle of wine and a brandy or two inside him, began telling tales of agents getting drunk on stake-outs and losing the car, reporting it stolen or sending in other agents the next day to investigate. Once an agent had managed to get transferred out of a partic-ularly onerous assignment only when he accidentally blasted a hole in the car's roof with the standard-issue shotgun, precipitating a rash of such accidents, first throughout the state, then on into Mississippi, Al-abama and beyond.

A painter of "how things might have happened in history" and (perhaps the most laid-back guy I'd ever seen) one who sold collectibles, Hopalong Cassidy lunchboxes, Gilbert erector sets and the like, in the weekend flea market downtown.

George, from whom knives protruded quill-like at boot top and waist (though our journalist suggested the knife handles might well be scarecrows, like those false beepers sold nowadays) and who ran a tattoo, excuse me, body art, shop out on the edge of Kenner. He'd been in the Quarter for a quarter of a century, a fixture there, till gentrifiers dragged him to the ground. No sense of tradition at all, those people, absolutely none at all—when tradition, that sense of history, is what made this city great. At one point, George said, better than 95 percent of prisoners had tattoos; from their body art you could tell within a year or so when the con had gone up on his first stretch, and where. Older, proletarian tattoos had always been formulaic, iconographic—blue dot, enwreathed heart, initials—while contemporary middle-class ones edged towards the pictorial and profuse. Might even say decadent. As a culture we've spent so long promoting hostility to whatever exists as the only honorable stand, too often hostility's all that's left, a bottle with nothing much inside. Still (George, hefting his mug of herb tea, asked us all) does anything better represent man's stubborn insistence to be himself and truly alive, to find beauty in the world and, if he can't find it, create it?

A rookie homicide detective, Angela, shaped like a barrel with eyebrows painstakingly plucked then drawn back in a high arch.

A thirtyish guy, Louis, Louie, maybe Luis, who'd just opened a bookstore specializing in used textbooks. School bookstores had long held an unchallenged monopoly, repurchasing texts again and again at bargain-basement prices and reselling them at penthouse premiums. It wouldn't last, he knew that, but for a while he'd be able dramatically to undercut the schools and still pull a fair profit. And even once this passed, he'd be left with the satisfaction of knowing he'd done good work—ah, America!

Dennis, bald except for a gray, limp ponytail sprouting off the back of his head, who taught drawing and design at three community colleges and served as part-time docent for the Delgado.

Danny and Steve. They ran an uptown B&B catering to gays and offered up, everyone said, breakfasts so good that guests got up an hour early just to enjoy them.

Phillip, who'd gone through the master's program in social work with Rick. He worked at the state hospital over in Mandeville, had for years.

Charles, a waiter at Petunia's who, whenever he was able to clear time, played clarinet with a local klezmer group, string bass with a pickup blues band meeting each weekend on Jackson Square. That group's washboard player frequently spilled out of her top. The group was very popular.

Towards ten that night, things began trailing off. God, we were old. Ten o'clock and the party's over. Pots of polenta gave out as had mushroom and roux earlier; plates of cheese, andouille sausage, toothpick-speared peppers and olives faded away; folks reaching into honeycombs of beer and wine bottles came up empty, which given our diminished tolerances was probably just as well. With Rick I saw the last few stragglers to the door, then put on Charlie Patton cranked high as we began stacking dishes, glasses, coffee cups, ashtrays.

"Thanks for letting me use your place, Lew."

"My pleasure. Great meal, fine company."

In the next room, slurring his words majestically (as I generally did these days, following the stroke), Patton saddled up his pony.

"You want, you're not into this right now, too tired to deal with it, we could leave it. I'd be glad to swing by early, before work, take care of it then."

"Just as soon get it done. I'm fine. Help me wind down some."

We worked away, Patton's guitar plucking at the edge of our world, calling up strong feelings I had no name for, feelings that, once summoned, I knew, would be slow to go away. Cleanup mostly done, we knocked off to share half a bottle of Australian Shiraz-cabernet I'd tucked away for safekeeping in the vegetable drawer, sitting together for the most part wordlessly, before Rick headed home. I was stacking a final few plates on towels, long ago bereft of drainer space, when the phone rang.

I made my way to it, shouted Hang on! Just a minute! and, carrying the phone with me, Deborah's cordless, went to turn down the music.

"Sorry."

A pause. "Mr. Griffin."

Maybe I should have left the music alone. Go back now and crank it up.

"I apologize for calling so late. I wanted to say how sorry I am to hear of your recent difficulties. . . . Our bodies *will* go on betraying us, won't they? Still, a stroke, if not too severe, can be an interesting thing. The jar gets shaken in intriguing ways. . . . You've made, I understand, a full recovery."

I wrung out the dishrag and draped it on the windowsill to dry. More accurately, probably, to mildew.

"I was pleased to hear that. If there's anything I can do . . . As you know, I've had considerable experience with this sort of thing these last several years. I would hope that you might call on me. Not that I think for a moment you will."

Time ticked in the wires.

"I am hardly a monster, Mr. Griffin. Few of us are. It's not as though I'm sitting here with drums going, waiting for those mighty gates to open."

"*I am a man, Jupiter.*"

"Ah yes. Sartre, to balance my own *King Kong*. Interesting, isn't it? How, increasingly, we seem to live our lives as allusion, reference—not directly, but refracted from something else."

The CD player had shut itself off, dropping the house into a supernal quiet.

"Thousands of years ago, Mr. Griffin. Thousands of years ago something, a creature who had not existed before, lugged itself up out of the slime and sat drying on a rock, looking around. It had no idea what it was, what it would become. Even where it was. But at that point, even with no words for it, the creature knew two things.

"It had knowledge of itself. It was self-aware.

"And it knew, as it struggled even to breathe in this new world, that it hurt."

Without response to that, I remained silent.

"Of course, personally, I have also the pragmatic, absolutely nonphilosophical consolation of knowing that, for me, the pain will soon be over. An unfair advantage, some might suggest."

"I'm sorry," I said after a moment.

"Why should you be? From your vantage, no doubt, I've earned my pain."

"We all do, in our own way. Just that sometimes it seems so out of proportion."

"Yes. Yes, sometimes it does." A cough started up in his chest, like a fist closing down; I heard him turn it away, end it, by sheer force of will. "I do apologize for calling so late."

"Not a problem."

"Good. . . . I should hate to impose." A man walked slowly past on the street outside, a step or so off the curb, looking in. He was shabbily dressed, eyes bright with something: drink, fever, too many lost battles, too much time alone. "I wonder if you may have given any further thought to what we last spoke of."

"Alouette, you mean."

"I suppose I do." When I said no more, he added: "She's well?"

"She is. As is the child."

"Good. Very good. And may I ask concerning the . . . notes . . . she has been receiving?"

"Dr. Guidry, I understand and appreciate your concern, but that's something you really need to take up with Alouette directly, not with me."

"You're right, of course. And I'd be happy to do so, if only she'd take my calls. At any rate, Mr. Griffin, forgive me. And thank you for your time, of which already I've taken up far too much."

"Not at all. Good night, sir."

I heard the receiver get set down and was about to hang up myself when a voice came on the line.

"Mr. Griffin, Catherine Molino here. You remember me?"

"Of course I do."

"Thank you for talking to him. He doesn't have much to look forward to these days. Perhaps . . ."

"Yes?"

"I was thinking that maybe someday it would be possible for you to come and see Dr. Guidry, speak to him about his daughter. That would mean a great deal to him."

"Why would I want to do that, Mr . Molino?"

She didn't speak for several moments. "Because he is old and sick and alone, Mr. Griffin. Or simply because we're all human."

Without waiting for a reply, she said, "Thank you, Mr. Griffin. Good night," and hung up.

22

I opened my eyes. Another eye hovered inches away, regarding mine. A rat. Its whiskers twitched. Obviously, whatever I was, I was too big to eat here. But he could go get help, haul me back home for later.

I sat up. Hard to believe what effort that took. For a moment the rat stood watching. But I was moving around now, no longer an easy target, alleyway carry-out. The rat moved off towards the wall, sniffing at better prospects there.

I was, indeed, in an alley. *I think we are in rat's alley where the dead men lost their bones.* But I wasn't dead. I wouldn't feel this bad if I were dead.

Yards off, doorway-size, an oblong of street and buildings showed. Light spilled from the doorway. Out there, cars passed, people hurried by on foot, life went on. Brick walls around me, a three-foot pile of black garbage bags, Dumpster marked Autumn House.

I felt at my pockets. Wallet gone. Money. One arm

of my sportcoat torn almost away, tie crushed, blood and dirt ground into my shirt, one shoe off and possibly gone missing.

Back home, on my own, I'd found the release and deliverance of literature. Here in the city I'd been introduced to another: alcohol. And I'd taken to it, as my father would have said, like a duck to water. *River was whiskey and I was a duck*, bluesman Buster Robinson sang, *I'd dive to the bottom and never come up.*

Bracing myself on the brick wall, I stood. Life's oblong there at the mouth of the alley wobbled and stood still. I staggered towards it. Last thing I could remember was this long conversation with a cabdriver in some anonymous bar off Canal, vague impressions of new rounds being ordered and other folk arriving and departing, among them two young women in town from Alabama who agreed to accompany us to the Seven Seas for a splash of true New Orleans. Then it all went blank.

Blanks and blurs were things I got used to.

I also got used to squad cars and cops asking questions.

"Bad night, boy?" one of them said. He stood, legs wide apart, just outside the alley. And barely out of high school from the look of him.

"You'd appear to be some beat up." That was the other one, hanging close by the car. Over the years, quantities of food dished up in New Orleans portions had made him a walking equator. Limp hair that looked like a fig leaf draped across his scalp. "You okay?"

I ducked my head, ambiguously. Could be agreeing, indicating I didn't know. Say as little as possible always: I'd learned that.

"Where you from?"

I tried, but for the life of me I couldn't come up with an address. Too many cheap apartments and rooms, the latest of them taken just a few days back. Some place off Jefferson, I thought.

"From the city, then."

"Like we didn't know?"

"Gonna take a little ride here."

Led to the car, I saw cement canals, establishments on the far shore. Metairie, then. Metairie cops were famous for picking up homeless and ferrying them back just across the line to New Orleans, dropping them there. Police equivalent of sweeping dirt under the rug. Threat dealt with. City's problem now.

Truth to tell, I fared little better back on familiar turf. Next time I woke, it was to similar environment and circumstances. The Metairie cops had dropped me off on Jefferson Highway and I'd started making my way towards home. Somewhere just the other side of Claiborne two guys came up and asked if I could help them with bus fare. They were pissed when I said I couldn't and *really* pissed when they found out I'd told them the truth and had nothing, no money, absolutely nothing of worth or use, on me.

"Sir, are you okay?"

From all evidence, no.

New Orleans's finest this time. Again I'm slumped up against a building somewhere and it's morning. Again I make it slowly to my feet.

23

"M AYBE you should call him."

"Maybe *you* should stop giving people advice."

Seven in the morning. Had I intentionally waited till I knew Larson would be gone, Alouette crowded for time?

"I'm sorry, Lew. That was uncalled for."

I shrugged.

"But you're right, these letters may be getting to me more than I admit, even to myself. Not that I understand why. There's really not much *there* there. Nothing substantial, no real menace, all implication—if even that." She paused. "Anyway, we've been out here on this train platform together before, Lewis. You can't fix the lives of everyone you care for. You should be paying attention to your own."

"I know."

"Of course you know." Her tone brought the word

exasperation to mind. "David's been gone how long now? What have you done about that?"

"He doesn't want to be found."

"Maybe not. But that begs the question, doesn't it? You love David. You don't want him out on the streets again."

"What I want isn't the important thing."

"You know what it's like, Lewis. You *know*."

I nodded.

"So instead, you set yourself on a crusade to run down this guy who's never done anything, who may just *possibly* be a stalker, but who might just as well be a good enough guy, maybe he's only a little slow, a little backwards. Or you go galumphing out on your horse to try and Sam Spade some pigeon killers. Desperate men for sure."

"I don't know . . . sometimes it's only when you don't look on directly that you're able to see a thing."

"True enough. And birds who don't find food for days at a time begin pecking up gravel and sand, preening themselves uncontrollably. It's called displacement behavior."

"Maybe you've been a social worker too long, dear."

"And you—"

"—too long a fuck-up?"

"Well. As a longtime social worker, of course, I'd prefer *troubled*. Or *conflicted*." She laughed. "Hold on a minute, the baby's crying." Not that shrill, fruit-bat cry you hear so often, but something at a lower pitch, human, authentic, that quickly subsided. Then Alouette was back. "For all of it, Lewis, you're still far and away the truest person I've known, and the kindest."

"I'd be flattered if it weren't for the fact that the work you do tends to limit exposure to possible competitors."

"There is that." She laughed again, a full-bodied,

rich, rolling laugh. Her mother's laugh. "And while I'd love to go on discussing philosophy with you, absolutely one of my favorite pastimes at seven in the morning, God knows, looking out on a brick wall with the smell of soiled diapers lugging up behind me, I really do have to get to work."

"We all have our burdens."

"Ah, yes. The many responsibilities our freedom entails. As that brick wall—I'm sure Heidegger and Sartre must point out somewhere—demonstrates."

I hung up the phone and carried mine (burdens, responsibilities) out to the kitchen like any good Southerner and, sitting at the table there, doused them with quantities of coffee. Times past, *dans le temps* as Vicky would put it, this is where we'd all gather, LaVerne and myself, Cherie, Clare, Don in the months he stayed with us, Alouette, David, half a dozen others over the years. Now I sat alone with haphazard hands of plates, cups and saucers dealt out across the Formica surface, brambles of cutlery, a jar of crystallized honey, plastic tumbler with half an inch of milk left at the bottom. Fanned beside them a week or two of mail. Pick a card. Electric, water and gas bills, lots of circulars, Visa, offers from video clubs, cable, Internet and other service providers, dues for the Authors Guild, plot rent for my parents' graves. Another stack of Deborah's working notes, which, though done with, would live here, I knew, until I found them new quarters. She'd left a note tacked to the fridge.

> Up with the birds.
>
> Sorry I was so late last night. Didn't want to wake you.
>
> Rehearsals are going well. Scarily well, actually. That feeling of what's happened here, it's got away from us all. But in the best possible way. (Still scary.)

Any chance you can mind the store today, maybe the next couple of days, afternoons?

We open this weekend. Can you believe it?

I'll grab breakfast out, probably just swing by McDonald's for a sausage biscuit. Not exactly Griffin fare, but hey.

Love you.

Hey.

Bat in his characteristic way suddenly appeared, leaping to the table, and sat watching me, tail sweeping slow, serpentine S's. Nothing's more important than the connections we make to others. It's all we have, finally. We move towards one another and away, close again, all these half-planned, intricate steps and patterns. Stand there far too often holding our bagloads of good intentions, shifting them from hip to hip, looking foolish.

Bat leaned onto his front legs and stretched, rump pushed up, to show what he thought of my reveries. .

By way of thanks, I fed him.

I may not have hobbled down to the park, but it felt like it. According to doctors and therapists, there were no sequelae from the stroke, only a little residual weakness, which was to be expected. Neither Deborah nor Don admitted to being able to see any compromise or debility, any change in the way I got around. But I'd go to push up out of a chair and find myself grabbing at things—not so much that I couldn't perform the physical act as that the world no longer represented itself to me as stable, dependable. I wondered if this was what Clare had felt, this pause, like a shield or a window, between intent and action, desire and spasm.

Lester sat looking out over the park, a sheen of

sweat, like varnish that hadn't taken, on the ma-
hogany of his forehead.

"Lewis," he said as I sank onto the bench beside
him. "How you doing?"

"Good enough, all things considered."

"You've been poorly then? Know I've missed seeing you."

I filled him in on my hospital stay.

He nodded. "Thing is, over the years you commence to spending so much time there, those hospital stays get to be like bus rides for you. Ain't the way
you'd *choose* to travel, but you know that's the only
way you're 'bout to get from one place to another
now."

We were all but alone in the park. A scatter of un-
familiar faces. I asked Lester about this.

"People done got scared, I think, some of them
anyway. Pondering if what killed them birds might not
just come after them 'n' their children next."

"The deaths haven't stopped, then?"

Lester nodded, not in agreement this time, indicating.

"Look at that sorry flock. What, ten or twelve
birds? And most of *them* gimped up one way or another. You remember how it used to be, Lewis. They'd
come in in swarms. Something startled them and they
took off, all those wings, it was like this sudden great
wind. They'd all but shut off the sun for a moment or
two." He sipped his drink, one or another of those
horribly sweet concoctions, Zima or such, pitched to
us blacks, and laughed. "'Course, this far along, remembering how things used to be starts looming large
for us, doesn't it? We don't be careful, that can get to
be *all* we think about."

He took another sip. The container hovered in
the hinterland between dumbbell- and vase-shaped,
label bright red and blue. Some sort of dog on it? A

naked woman? Could even be a truck. "You ever tried this shit?"

I shook my head.

"Don't."

The hand holding the abomination lifted, two ruler-long fingers unfurling.

"Walk over to the other side of those bushes, Lewis, and you'll come across a fair stretch of grave sites. Lots of birds been laid to rest back there. We put them in the ground ourselves, the boy and me. Just a few at first, then sometimes, later on, as many as three or four a day. With whatever ceremony we could manage."

He put the container, mostly empty, on the bench beside him. A group of Hispanic teens sat together atop a slide, stretch of dark midriff showing between the girl's sweater and skirt, guys exhibiting their own brand of midriff: two inches or so of boxer shorts peeked out over low-slung denims. Thirty degrees out and they've got skin showing. Tough kids.

"Boy won't come with me anymore," Lester said. "Almost got him here a couple of times. Tell him we were going for a walk, maybe we'd stop off for dough-nuts after. But then he'd see where we were going and commence to crying and shaking. You remember how much he loved being here, Lewis. It's a sad thing, truly sad. Boy don't have much. His room, the park. Now half that's got taken from him."

Lester sat shaking his head. "Maybe there really *isn't* any more to it. Maybe it *don't* make sense and ain't meant to. Vanity and vexation of the spirit, just like it says in Ecclesiastes."

He laid a hand on my knee and I found myself wondering if in all these years we'd ever before touched. Surely we'd at least shaken hands. Right: that single, pained handshake.

"Good seeing you again, Lewis. Good that you're up and about again, too."

"That's a lot of goods for someone quoting Ecclesiastes, downer of all downers, just moments ago."

"What can I say?" The hand came up off my leg; those impossibly long fingers unfolded in the space before us and moved there expressively, putting me in mind of branches in gentle wind, of Dante: Half into life's journey I came to myself within a dark wood where the straight way was lost. "It's a character flaw. Try as I will, no matter how I practice and worry over it, I simply can*not* stay glum for very long." He pushed himself up off the bench. "I'd best be getting back to the boy now."

I said good-bye, that I'd see him soon.

"Maybe, if you found time, you might even come see the boy again? I think, when you did, that was good for him. I noticed a difference just after."

"I'll plan on it, then."

He looked off momentarily, adrift on his own thoughts. "Good."

The teens, when I approached them, had some trouble deciding between wary, smart-ass or antagonistic as best response. One of the boys popped the joint they'd been sharing into his mouth and swallowed.

"¿Que hay?" I asked. "¿De dónde son?"

Whatchu care? one of the kids wanted to know.

I told them.

"That boy? We seen him, sure. He ain't right."

They went in and out of Spanish as they spoke.

"Always with that same old man you been sittin' wif."

To them I was just one of a string of old guys without a clue. At worst a cop, child welfare agent or some other meddler from the outside world, otherwise someone inconsequential, and in either case so far outside the orbit of their lives as scarcely to exist. The Spanish helped. I didn't come within a mile of speaking it well but, thanks to Rick Garces, on a good day with the wind blowing my way, I could fake it.

Guardedly they allowed as how, yeah, man, they were here most days, so? Had they taken any notice of the pigeons? Rats, they said, rats with wings, that's what we call them.

There used to be a lot of them.

Sure did.

But now there's only a handful left.

He's right, they told one another.

"Someone's been poisoning them."

The teens had stopped looking back and forth among themselves. Now they all looked at me. What they want to do that for? one asked. Yeah, don't kill nothin' you don't plan to eat.

"Cases like this," I said, "usually it's someone from the neighborhood. Someone with a grudge, some private agenda. Maybe they've been hanging around, on the edge of things, face at the back of the crowd you never quite notice."

Hey man, we don't notice, how we goan tell you bout it?

Good point.

'Sides, it ain't like we spend the day here.

Yeah, we be out here during lunch and once school lets out.

But that's it for us, mister, we got other things to do. What's that word you used? Agendas.

Fuck agendas, man.

Yeah, we got lives.

Gracias, I told them. Gracias por su ayuda.

De nada.

Hey, one of them called out, this time in English,

as I turned. You need to talk to Mister Bones. He *always* here.

And it turned out that he was, though in all these years I'd never seen him. If I had, I'd have remembered, what with chicken bones through septum and earlobes African fashion and an Amerind-style breastplate of the same. If this had been a cartoon, some toothy black man would be doing a Lionel Hampton on those. Mister Bones never came in the park—something bad had happened here long past, he told me later—but neither was he ever far away. Mostly he resided under the porch of the abandoned house opposite. Had a mattress, most of a sleeping bag, boxes of canned and dry goods down there. Or else, when things got wet, he'd make his way up into the tree house some kids had built half a century back and half a block down in a massive water oak.

Today, as usual, he was under the house. I shouted ahead then started under myself, thinking how my grandfather, working as builder, spent much of his life crawling under houses like this, crippled leg and all, fitting pipe, splicing wire, shoring foundations.

Somewhere in the back of my mind I had to be wondering, too, just what the hell I was doing. Alouette was right. My son had disappeared, my goddaughter was receiving anonymous threats, I'd just got scraped up off the floor with the medical equivalent of a spatula—and here I was, fifty-odd years old, snaking under a house to try and find out who's been killing pigeons. Strange life all around.

"You the tax man," he said, "or one of Mr. Hoover's minions, you just might as well go on back out of here, and fast."

I told him who I was.

"Lew Griffin." He grunted. "Think I may've done heard some 'bout you."

"Oh?"

"Damn, man, this here ain't nothing but a over-grown small town. Ever'body know your business. You bring trouble."

"Got a load with me now, in fact. Thought you might help put me together with the people who need it."

"So they live happily ever after."

"Something like that."

"Ain't got much truck with other folks' needs. Not a one of them's ever he'ped me much."

"I know that."

"Think you know a lot, don't you?" Someone was walking on the porch floor above us. Their floor, our roof. Rotted from rain, desiccated from heat, boards creaked, went swayback and threatened to give way. "But look at you. Come crawling up under here like some goddamn kid looking for answers, still think the world *got* answers for you. Ain't no fortune cookies, you know. Break'm open, read what to do in there."

We listened as footsteps paced back and forth above.

"Cold as a sonuvabitch down here," I said.

"You get used to it after a time. Year or two. I been down here—hell, I don't know how long I been down here. Man gets used to 'most anything. . . . You feelin' trollish?"

"I don't know what I'm feeling. Not my feet. And the fingers are going fast."

"Shiiii. You a part-timer." That was funny enough to say again. "Part-timer."

"More ways than one," I admitted. "But you're not. And I figure you have to have seen my boy over there in the park."

"One they call Dog Boy."

"Yes."

"I've seen him all right. Seen you with him, too."

"Then you know how much he loves life."

"I know how much he loves animals."

"There's a difference?"

Mister Bones shrugged. His breastplate rattled like Venetian blinds in wind.

"Someone's been killing pigeons. Poisoning them."

"Sure have. For a time now . . . You okay under here? You don't look too comfortable. Noticed a blanket set out to dry on a porch across the way yesterday, probably still be there. We could go get that for you."

Moments limped by.

"I want to find them. The ones who are doing it."

"They're survivors, you know. Pigeons. You have to respect that."

Even though he was looking out towards the park and couldn't see me, I nodded.

"Like us," he said. "You hungry, Griffin? Miz Miller up the way left a can of Vienna sausages out on the stoop for me last night. Be happy to share them with you, you want."

24

THE stairway stank of urine, beer, stale cigarette smoke and mold. Once, long in the past, there'd been carpeting. Fragments of green remained in patches, mostly beneath nailheads, like tufts of hair sprouting from old men's ears. As I entered, someone let loose a bowl of water from the third landing, screaming *I told you not to come back here, goddamn it!* No one else on the stairway as the cascade came down and I ducked aside. A door slammed.

Each floor held six apartments, *A* through *F*, though in no apparent order. *A* might just as easily be the apartment nearest the stairs, or tucked away between *E* and *B*. A pencil eraser would have taken down most of the doors. Walls bore deep gouges, long troughs, as though trucks had been driven repeatedly into them over the years. Here and there plaster had come away in great statuelike chunks; elsewhere it clung on bravely. At one turning I put my hand against the wall and precipitated an avalanche of plaster nuggets, pebbles, powder. This went on for some time. Stairwell corners held stacks of gravid boxes, belongings for which residents had no room inside, presumably. Surprising that these hadn't long ago been borne off. Posters of Sixties movies and rock shows hung alongside paintings of clowns and seascapes on landings. The whole stairway creaked and swayed like a suspension bridge.

I climbed to the fourth floor. Four's about as far as it goes for most of New Orleans, outside downtown anyway. The city's well below sea level, filled-in swampland for the most part, one of those triumphs of man's imagination and will that the world periodically refutes with such rejoinders as floods and hurricanes. Then I came to 4-A.

This door wasn't going to be taken down with an eraser. It fit the frame flush. No give to it, no space about the edges, no apparent weak spot. Door and frame both steel.

I knocked. It was like rapping knuckles on a boulder. Whole armies could be on the move in there, tanks, armored vehicles, transports, and I wouldn't hear them.

Incredibly enough, the door opened.

A thirtyish man in cornrows wearing Tommy Hilfiger's clothes, barrel-like shorts, oversize rugby-style shirt (I hoped Tommy had more), stood there. Skin color medium brown, eyes blue-gray. Brows and upper lip lifted at the same time, three birds taking flight.

"Those our bitches?" someone behind him said.

"Sure nuff don't look to be," the doorman said. Then to me: "What*chu* want?"

Taking that as an invitation, I pushed my way in. Doorman fell back, then recovered and came towards me, leg lifting for a karate kick. When the ankle came up, I grabbed it and twisted as I shoved it towards the ceiling, hammered a fist into his crotch. He went down as the others shot up off the couch.

I'd taken notice of the rock sitting by the door as I entered. Judging from roundness and polish, it had spent several human lifetimes in water somewhere perfecting itself. About the size of an orange and used as a doorstop, no doubt. The one who'd come up off the couch and started towards me went down hard when it hit him square in the forehead. I'd thrown underhanded, like a kid on a softball team. That left two of us on opposite banks with the river of a sky-blue couch between. This one was older, done up in high grunge: plaid shirt with sleeves flapping, long-sleeved T-shirt under, cord jeans bagged into camel's knees and shiny with wear. Both hands came up, palm out. He stepped out from behind the couch shaking his head.

"Whatever this is, man—"

"You live here?"

He shook his head again.

"Then what are you doing here?"

"Guess I'd best be asking myself that same question 'long about now." He looked down at the floor, from one to the other of the bodies there, then back at me. "Thing is, I went to high school with Pryor here, guy making that snoring sound? Not that we ever hung out back then, nothin' like that. But this morning when I ran up against 'im at Hoppin Jon's, suddenly he's acting like we're old-time bros."

Picking up on my unvoiced question, he said: "It's a bar and grill just off Claiborne downtown. Serves a kickin' breakfast, so lots of night workers turn out, hospital workers, firemen, paramedics going off duty, camp followers. I pull graveyard shift at the coroner's myself, have for years. So I'm sitting at the bar, just gonna have a quick one and head out, when Pryor comes up and says, Hey man, I know you. This here's Levon, he tells me, my boy. We had a few drinks, scored breakfast, wound up back here. Next thing I know, you're busting in."

He still had his hands up. Now slowly he put them down.

"This over, man—or you just puttin' in a new clip? Anything I can do to help convince you to let me walk out of here?"

"That could happen." Briefly I told him what brought me there, about the boy, the dead pigeons.

"This bone man's the one gave them up?"

"He sees everything that goes on in the park. One day these two, never been regulars before, take to hanging 'round, and they get to be like toothaches, just won't go away. Turn up in the park with paper bags too small for lunches, anything like that, and leave empty-handed. Them boys weren't proper, he said. Knew it from the first."

"Proper?"

"What he said."

"Well, they're definitely bent. He got that right."

"Finally one day he hauled himself out from under the house and followed them back here. Never did nothin' like that before, he told me. Ain't likely to again."

"Not your typical concerned citizen."

"Not the kind you usually hear about, anyway."

We stood silently with that river of a couch beside us, bodies washed up on its shore. Behind him a diminutive arch showed a swatch of pinkish hallway.

"Anyone else back there?"

"Pretty sure not."

"What is?"

He shrugged.

"Let's go see."

The hallway was about the size of a large man's coffin. Bathroom directly ahead, bedrooms at either end. Barely enough wall space for the doors. We went left.

"Holy shit!" my companion said.

The entire back wall was paved with bird's wings, single wings nailed there and spread, all at the same attitude and angle, one after another, a hundred or more. Like fish scales, covering the wall completely, floor to ceiling. Against the wall opposite, fifty or sixty cheap wooden cages were stacked. These contained the skeletons of birds.

I stood in the middle of the room trying to imagine such cruelty: where it would come from, why and how it would take this form. Had a vision of them starting out catching the pigeons, in the park or elsewhere, putting them in cages just to watch them starve to death. Then moving on to poisoning and scalping—collecting the wings we saw here. Finally letting the birds lie where they fell.

"You ever in the service?" my companion said.

"Yeah. Not long, though."

"See action?"

"Not the usual sort."

"You were lucky."

I nodded.

"Me, I thought anything had to be better than watching my old lady toss that same coin in the air every night, wait to see whether she'd kill herself with the drugs first or get killed by some scumball she brought home. I was sixteen. By the time I was seventeen and threw away my helmet, I'd drunk sixty or eighty cases of beer and thought the world was mine, you know? Drop me anywhere, desert, jungle, I'd *take* the damn place, it belonged to me. That was an attitude rankers could get behind. So off I went to ranger school. Picked up some skills there that don't do a lot for my résumé."

We were back in the front room by this time.

"Only place I ever saw anything like that," he said, indicating the trophy room. "We're cool, you and me?"

I nodded.

"Anything else you need here?"

Levon had pushed himself over to the wall and partway up it and leaned there clutching his privates. Pryor, turned facedown, was trying to get to his feet, pointed toes of his Western boots scratching at the floor.

"Think I'll stick around a while, then, have a talk with these boys. Like in the old days. Put some of those skills the government taught me back to work? Recycle them, like."

I kept expecting to come across a story about guys nailed to the wall, arms at least, but I never did.

That afternoon I stopped off at a friend's place up on Carrollton. June Bug, everybody called him, another vet. He lived in a lean-to on the flat roof of an apartment house up that way, on a floor of tar that gradually liquefied as the day progressed, and he raised pigeons.

"Name's Mr. Blue," June Bug told me as we peered into the cage. I'm not sure I ever realized just how many shades of blue there are. The pigeon's head was such a dark blue that it caught light and shone. Cerulean tipped its wings. Individual feathers were here dark, there light, powder blue, azure, aquamarine, indigo, no two of them alike. "And don't you go tryin' to change it, neither. Real thoroughbred, ain't he?" The pigeon peered back out at me, cocking its head the way they do. Who the hell was I and what was I doing hanging around outside its cage? I'd brought a bottle of cheap brandy along. Mr. Blue and I left that and a fifty-dollar bill behind.

Dog Boy's eyes when I introduced them were all I'd ever need as thanks. I'd stopped off at a pet shop on the way to pick up food, treats, cage-size avian equivalents of parallel bars and vaulting horses. You give someone a pigeon, you want it to be a fit pigeon. Mr. Blue looked every bit as pleased as the boy.

"Thank you, Lewis," Lester said. I'd been doing my best to shuttle off unseen down the stairs, but Lester came hobbling after me. "Hope it makes a difference," I told him.

I'd barely got home—to an empty house again, but no matter—when a call from Lester asserted that indeed it *had* made a difference. The boy's up, moving around, he said, for the first time in weeks. "He and Mr. Blue are sitting by the window in his room, looking out. It's a sight."

The next call was from Don.

I'd managed to get out most of the first syllable, "Hel—" before he started in.

"How much you know about this Guidry character?"

"Don. Good to hear from you. I've been fine. And you? Jeeter fitting right in, Jeanette okay with it, they're getting along?"

Silence at the other end.

Finally: "You through?"

"I guess."

"So what *do* you know about Guidry?"

"Not a lot. Some kind of doctor, though I'm not sure he ever had much of a practice. He did have connections, though. Old money, I assumed. That whole underground Creole-society thing."

"What I'm wondering about here is previous marriages—before LaVerne."

"None that I know of. But you pretty much know what I know. He treasured Alouette."

"So did LaVerne. Enough that, just to stay with her, she allowed her own life to be completely taken over by him."

"True enough."

"Guidry was well along in years when he and LaVerne hooked up. You think the wick stayed dry all those years?"

"Probably not, but—"

"No fucking way."

For a moment I thought I heard steps on the porch. "Okay. So why do I get the feeling this conversation has suddenly gone multiple choice?" Key in the lock? Deborah? David? No. Just this old house breathing.

"Not that I have much of anything," Don said. "Lots of blanks that need filling in. Like all our lives. Years of monthly payments stretching back to the Seventies, for instance—to Gladstone Hall, whatever that is. And something that looks suspiciously like a trust fund, though so far I haven't been able to get in close enough for a good look. Administered by Guidry's lawyers, at any rate. Firewalls thick all around. I'll keep chipping away. Rick's on it, too."

He paused.

"You okay, Lew?"

"Tired. A little the worse for wear." I filled him in on the party scene back at apartment 4-A.

"Getting kinda long in the tooth for that kind of action, my friend."

"Tell me about it."

"You need me to come over there?"

"What for? Party's over."

"You don't sound real good."

"Nothing a few hours' sleep won't help. Say twelve or fourteen? I'll talk to you tomorrow."

"You sure?"

"I'm sure."

We went back and forth a couple times more before hanging up. I snagged a Shiraz-cabernet blend from the kitchen pantry and sat by the front window, level of wine in the bottle and daylight outside falling at pretty much the same pace. I thought about Dog Boy and Mr. Blue sitting by their window watching this same night fall. Wondered if David might be looking out a window somewhere, where that might be if so, and what *he* might be thinking. Then, for whatever reason, I found myself struggling to recall ambition, wondering just why, year after year, I'd gone on pushing my way through all those cases, gone on fighting so hard for a handful of lost and damaged people, why I'd sunk myself and so much of my life into a handful of peripheral, forgotten books.

Light and wine both gone, I left those emptinesses behind and took my own upstairs to bed.

I was in a library and the library was on fire. I grabbed books at random off the shelves, stuffing them underarm. Had to save what I could, as many as I could. Down a corridor towards me strolled James Joyce, tip of a handsome malacca cane tapping the floor in front of him, shoes buffed to a high polish but severely down at the heels, eyes huge behind glasses. "Is there, sir, a problem?" The elevator door opened. Borges stood inside. His useless, boiled-egg eyes swept over me. He wore a well-appointed three-piece pinstripe suit, one black shoe, one brown. "Milton," he said, "has anyone seen John Milton? He was just here. We were talking." I scuttled towards the stairway, books spilling from my arms. . . .

Whereupon the library's fire alarm there in that fanciful land became my telephone here in this unregenerate one.

And whereupon, when my arm appeared to ignore the message sent it—simple enough directions, after all: reach out, pick up the phone—I panicked. I knew this lag, this recalcitrance. I'd had another stroke, and a worse one this time, no doubt about it. What should be currents pulsing down the wires of nerves had become a spray of welder's sparks. Everything got worse. Always. The world's single immutable law.

But in fact the arm had only fallen asleep. Seconds later (though at the time it seemed far longer) the arm responded. I watched as, pins and needles firing along its length, it followed through. Found the phone, fetched it to me. Still felt as though my shoulder had two or three pounds of dead meat strapped to it. Then tongue and palate repeated the misfire.

"Lew?" Deborah said in response to my *gaugh?*

I tried again, coming up with, approximately, *Yegguh*.

"Lew, are you all right?" Alarm in her voice now.

Swallowing, clearing my throat. Trying out a few vowels and diphthongs offstage, then swinging the mouthpiece back towards me. Humming, I remembered reading somewhere, humming was supposed to relax your vocal cords.

"Lew, what are you doing? What the hell is that?"

"Humming."

"Humming. As in bird."

"Right: humming pigeon. Humming relaxes the vocal cords. Like doing warm-ups, stretches."

"But you're all right."

"I'm fine. Sorry. It's been a tough day. I was flat out, dreamless." No way I'd tell her just *how* tough it had been, or why. "What time is it?"

Silence on the line. Finally: "We've been together what, four or five years now, Lew?"

"Something like that."

"You have any idea how often, in all those years, you asked me the time?"

"No."

"Never. Not once. Clocks, dates, time of day, none of that ever had much to do with the way you live your life."

Which, upon reflection, was probably true, and I had to wonder, as she did, why now such things should matter. Hand meanwhile had distinguished itself from phone and begun its climb back up the phylogenetic slope. Switching the phone to the other, I shook the left heartily, worked it as though pumping the bulb of a sphygmomanometer that (I had little doubt) would reveal a dramatically elevated blood pressure. Like many things in life, alcohol for instance, relationships, or writing books, the meds had worked for a while, then stopped working.

"Still at rehearsal?"

"Not really—though there's a chance we might go back. That's why I'm calling." She waited and, when I said no more, went on. "You sure you're okay, I don't need to come home?"

"I'm sure."

"Okay."

Crackles and pops in the wire.

"Things haven't been going too well for us lately. That's not exactly news, I guess. A lot of it's my fault. I wanted so badly to find some way off the track. And now I've been so immersed in getting the play done. When I have coffee, whether or not I eat or sleep, deliveries at the store, sales there, regular hours—none of that seems to matter much anymore. I used to feel like this a lot, Lew. All the time. I wasn't sure I ever would again."

More crackles and pops. Light from outside fell through the window, pushing a slab of brightness into place on floor and wall, darkening the rest of the room.

"Never easy, is it?" I said.

"No reason it should be."

We stood poised on parallel wires, balance poles like cats' whiskers out at our sides.

"You have somewhere to stay?"

"Temporarily. . . . I'm sorry, Lew."

"Me too."

"I love you, you know."

"Yes."

I hung up the phone. From nowhere Bat appeared, leaping onto the nightstand. He sat there, eyes fixed upon me, purring, then collapsed, paws hooked over the edge. Telling me another life was there alongside my own, that I wasn't alone after all.

25

THANK you for coming. Can Mrs. Molino get you anything? Coffee? Something to eat, perhaps. A sandwich? We've just received a fine Virginia ham—shipped in from North Carolina, not Virginia, as it happens. Or since we're well along in the afternoon, perhaps a single malt. Some years ago you had, as I remember, a taste for Scotch."

"Taste had little to do with it."

"So I understood at the time."

My eyes were on Catherine Molino, standing near the door through which I'd entered. What looked to be an original Ingres floated above her left shoulder, a framed Picasso drawing, four abrupt lines coming together in the most improbable manner, at her right. Black, Oriental-looking hair gathered in a clip at the base of a swanlike neck. Designer jeans and a man's white dress shirt with sleeves rolled, tails out, handmade brocade vest over.

"I'm good, thank you."

Mrs. Molino smiled, nodded once and withdrew. Smile, nod and withdrawal all equally engaging.

"Alouette, I take it, proved otherwise occupied and unable to accompany you?"

"I saw no reason to ask—as I'm sure you understand."

"Of course."

Looking far too small for it, Guidry sat in an antique highback wheelchair, as though the chair with time might be diminishing him, gaining by increments some stature drained from him. The room was warm enough to have orchids sprouting from cracks in the walls; nonetheless a blanket covered lap and legs.

"An old man's blood goes thin," he said as I took off my coat, "turns from wine to water," and hung the coat across the back of my chair.

Here, we were well apart from the world I watched go on about its business outside the window. Everything in the room, carpet, curtains, walls, blanket, was blue-green, and all of it seemed slightly out of focus, fluid, shimmering. Here we moved at a much slower pace than those out there in that other world.

I'm underwater. This room's an aquarium.

"Once again, Mr. Griffin, I thank you for coming. You had little enough reason or inclination to do so."

"True."

"So why *have* you come?"

"To be quite honest, Dr. Guidry—"

"Horace. Please."

"—I'm not sure. I've nothing to offer. Nor is there anything I want from you."

"Of course."

We sat quietly a moment. Half a block away, girls in plaid skirts and white shirts with pocket crests pumped swings higher and higher while young men in charcoal slacks and white shirts with clip-on ties shot baskets. All of this soundless outside the aquarium walls.

Turn off sound and even the most familiar scenes, the commonest human gestures, turn strange on you. Not to mention what strange lives these were to me in the first place, how impenetrable. Nothing whatsoever to do with my own. I might as well be watching lobster or rays in their tanks. Ant farms. Beehives.

"Just felt I should be here, I guess."

"Intuition. Much of your life has been shaped by it."

"What shape there's been, yes."

"And not always to your benefit."

That, too, I had to concede.

"Still you persist."

I shrugged. "As good a guide as any other, finally."

"Anything can save you if you grab it hard enough, and hold on." He smiled. "You're surprised that I've read your books."

"I'm surprised *anybody's* read them. Surprised they were ever written, for that matter."

"But surely you must realize their attraction. How they take up the common textures of our lives—"

"And just what do you think might be common in the textures of our lives, Doctor Guidry?"

He paused. "You're right, of course. A presumption on my part. Forgive me. Nonetheless, taking the books' own high ground—scrambling for their shelter, if you like—I have to tell you I found them fascinating. Those first sentences drew me in. I was *there*. Oil pumps shushing Lew as he stands waiting to kill a man, water oak splitting open like a book in the storm. Lew himself shot, coming half-to there in the emergency room."

"Parent searching for a lost child."

"Yes."

Hands emerged from beneath the blanket and found their way to wheels, swiveling the chair to see what it was I watched over his shoulder. Wrists looked frozen, immobile, knots of bone protruding like cypress roots, fingers swollen and red as sausages. "Young people. . . . We should never let ourselves get too far away from them." Then, swiveling the chair back around: "It's not just another Catholic school, you know—despite the uniforms. Private, yes. But there's no church affiliation. None. Other parts of the nation, they call it a magnet school. Culling the most talented, most promising students from *all* the city's schools, small and large and in between, bringing them together here. I'm privileged to contribute."

Bending, he plucked a catheter bag from the side of the wheelchair, snapped his finger against the valve at the top, waited a moment, then snapped again. Bright gold fluid flowed into the bag in a gush. He let go of the bag and it swung there at the end of its rubbery placenta, back and forth.

"I know about David, of course."

I nodded.

"Recently I called to ask if you'd consider finding someone for me."

"And I declined."

"You did, yes. And it's a capacity in which I require you no longer."

One hand snaked out again from beneath the blanket. A crooked finger hovered. Was I to follow knuckle, first joint, or tip? Each pointed in a different direction.

"There's a folder on the desk, at the corner there. Perhaps you'd be so good as to retrieve it?"

I did so.

"Therein are copies of letters I've received. They may prove of interest."

Opening the folder, I read the top page and the one under, then shuffled through the rest, perhaps a dozen of them. Each began with some variation of history asserting itself. Memory transports us . . . In those years . . . Experience shows that . . . Those who have no knowledge of history are doomed to repeat it. Santayana I took as a bad sign. This went on, soon enough we'd be getting Shakespeare and Ross Macdonald, quotes from Tocqueville manhandled like soft clay into shapes their author never intended.

"I can keep these?"

He nodded. The nod was easier than pulling out of it. Gravity and time are toll bridges, fares keep going up.

"You know who sent them."

He started to say more but stopped himself.

"No."

"A moment ago you spoke as though you did."

His eyes went from the wall where they'd wandered, back to me. They were amazingly clear. "At first . . ." Blue springwater tumbling over white stone. "But what I thought then, upon first seeing them, I know can't possibly be true. You've had a chance to look them over now, Mr. Griffin. What do they suggest to you?" His head dipped an eighth of an inch.

"Aside from the fact that you're withholding information, you mean."

One diffident hand made its way to the surface, floated there a moment with fingers together like logs in a raft—confirming? allaying?—then subsided. Guidry's chin followed the hand down to sink onto his chest, bisecting the curve. He snored.

I eased from the chair and made my way into the outer room. Guidry's home had been built around the turn of the century as Europeans began taking over the city and crept by degrees uptown, putting up ever more magnificent homes in rivalry to those of downtown Creoles. At one point, like many others, the home had been transformed, to a hotel in this case, but unlike others suffered few structural modifications. This outer room, originally intended as parlor or sitting room, in its hotel period a lobby, had remained much the same through all the home's avatars.

Mrs. Molino rose from behind an elegant antique desk that put one in mind of stilt-legged birds.

"He's asleep," I said.

She nodded.

"For much of the day. And careening about the past the remainder. There's not a lot left to him. Or of him. We always think of the elderly as increasingly needy, but it's quite the opposite, really. Their lives get simpler—attain a kind of purity. There's little enough now that I can do for the doctor. I manage his affairs, offer what comfort I can. Just as you've done. Thank you again for coming."

"I'm not sure why I did, or, for that matter, what good it may have done. But you're welcome."

"Mr. Griffin?" she said behind me.

I turned.

"He's concerned over the letters, isn't he? The messages Alouette has been receiving."

"Should he be?"

She stepped briskly across the room to stand close. Tall and slender, man's oversize white dress shirt billowing out in the breeze of her passage, making me remember the first time I saw Deborah there beside the counter in her shop and thought *willowy*, as I'd done so often since. No sign of internal struggle in her eyes.

"That's not for me to say."

I could smell the shampoo she'd used that morning, apples and pears, a quiet tide of garlic, olive and lemon on her breath. Massively unsure of myself and long out of practice, signals a blur, I asked if she might consider having dinner with me. Or just coffee, if she'd be more comfortable with that.

I've embarrassed her, I thought at first; then, as she regained composure, recognized her reaction for what it was: some essential core of shyness overcome but unvanquished. Her eyes met mine.

"Understand that it's terribly difficult for me to get away . . ."

I nodded.

"But yes. Yes, I'd like that very much, Mr. Griffin."

"Good."

"You have my number. Please call. We'll arrange something."

Touching her lightly on the upper arm, I took my leave.

From a phone in a K&B just down the street I dialed her number. New-fashioned teenagers sat with piercings and bleached hair behind old-fashioned stemmed glasses of cherry phosphate and malted milk at the lunch counter. A hunched, rickety man pushed himself erect before the display of condoms, natural vitamins and copper bracelets to brace the harried pharmacist over conflicting needs and insurance plan, his wheelchair's E-cylinder of oxygen a silent witness.

"Mr. Griffin calling about those arrangements," I said, "could you please hold?"

She laughed. "Certainly. This *is* a bit earlier than I'd expected to hear from him. Will you tell Mr. Griffin that?"

"I will indeed. Anything else I should tell him?"

"Well . . . There's a good chance I'd be ready by seven, if he happened by. And a fair chance, too, that reservations might be waiting for us at Commander's."

"Seven. Commander's. Got it. And who is this again?"

The connection went. She would have set the phone gently in its cradle. Smiling.

26

ORNING'S his best time, Catherine Molino
said of Guidry. And my worst.

That particular morning, after returning to
the house, drinking a pot of coffee and reading deeply
into Rimbaud, I pulled my detective out of the box in
which he'd rested peacefully for years, propped him
up and set him to work, writing in his guise, there at
the kitchen table as I looked past sink and sill and recalled a stream of cheap apartments:

> My room looks out on a garden. There are enor-
> mous trees beneath my narrow window. At three
> in the morning, the candlelight grows dim and
> all the birds start singing at once in the trees.
> No more work. I gaze at trees and sky, transfixed
> by that inexpressible first hour of morning. I can
> see the school dormitories, completely silent.
> And already I hear the delicious, resonant, clat-
> tering sound of carts on the boulevards.

I have another drink and spit on the roof-tiles—because my room is a garret. Soon I'll go down to buy bread. It's that time of day. Workers are up and about all over the place. I'll have a drink or two at the corner bar, come back to eat my bread and leftovers, be in bed by seven, when the sun brings woodlice out from under the roof-tiles.

Early mornings in summer and December evenings—these are what I remember, what I love most about this place I find myself.

I paused, changed the period to a comma, and added:

this place where I've fallen to earth anew.

Just what had prompted me to carry this away from my reading of Rimbaud? Why, of all things, candles? And, given that my books were set in New Orleans, surely the woodlice should be roaches—of the hearty species that, as one local friend notes with more than a touch of pride, rock you back on your heel when you step on them? But something had caught, and this wouldn't be like other times I'd sat at the table scribbling. These pages wouldn't go onto the heap of bills, junk mail and newspapers on the shelf by the table, by the Mason jar stuffed full of corks from wine bottles and the mug with its stub of a handle like a broken tooth and its cargo of buttons, paper clips, corroded copper pennies, dimes worn smooth. These pages would be, as they grew, my last book, a return to where it all started.

When the phone rang, levering me back into *this* world, I looked up in surprise. The clock on the stove read 1:13. Had I always known it was there? Small engines go on ticking everywhere about us.

Four calls all told, that afternoon.

The first was from Jeanette asking Deborah and me to dinner with her, Don and Derick that night. Kind of a celebration, she said. Though of what, they hadn't decided yet. Maybe we could all do that together, decide.

"Thanks, Jeanette, but incredibly enough you've caught me on one of those rare evenings—these occur maybe two or three times a year—when I actually have plans."

"Well, we're sorry, of course. But we can do this later."

"That would be great. As long as it's not too much trouble."

"We have dinner most nights, Lewis."

"True enough. But you don't celebrate every night."

She paused before saying, "In our own way, I think we do."

"There's something else, Jeanette."

I told her about Deborah's departure.

"I'm so sorry, Lew. Are you okay?"

"I will be, sure."

"If there's anything we can do . . ."

"Thanks."

"We'll talk soon."

"You bet."

I'd barely made it back to kitchen, chair and legal pad before the phone rang again. I sat looking through the open doorway at the phone on its table, newel post, wooden floor, the pattern of it. A composition, like Van Gogh's painting of his room at Arles, something brought to stillness and no longer quite of this world.

"I'll be there in ten minutes," Don said when I picked up.

"No need, my friend."

"Fifteen at the outside."

"Do us all a great favor, Don. Stay home with your family. It's cold out. And I'm fine."

"Sure you are."

"Really. I am."

"You sure?"

"It's not exactly like I was blindsided, is it? This's been working its way to the surface for a long time."

"And nothing you could do about it, I suppose."

Little moved on street and sidewalk, lawns, porches. Every minute or two, as though chugging across a TV screen, exhaust a white plume, a car traversed the window. Two kids on collapsible scooters with bright green wheels rowed by. Had the neighborhood ever been this quiet, this still, by day? The cold was a part of it. But I had again the eerie, familiar feeling that there'd been some catastrophe, some dislocation, which only I and a handful of others had survived.

"How many times have we been through this, Lew, your side or mine?"

"Too many."

"Both of us lost count some years back, I guess."

"Probably just as well."

"Yeah." Behind him I heard the sounds of life going on: voices, rattle of cutlery and dishes, drawers, cabinets, a radio or TV. "Angels die. Because the air's too thick for them down here. *Skull Meat*."

"Or *The Old Man*. One of them, anyway."

"You always disparage your books, Lew, pretend they aren't important to you. I never have understood that."

"They're important—if that's the right word— while I'm writing them. Afterwards . . ." Afterwards, what? "They're pretty much a blur to me. One runs into another." Like our lives here on the island. Scatter of bright segments, the rest of it mush.

Another of those comfortable silences that existed between Don and myself from the first, and that increasingly with the years seemed to occupy our time together, fell.

"Okay, so I'll stay home," Don said finally. "But only if you promise to call if you need me, man. A drink, a meal, just to talk."

"Absolutely."

The third call came within the hour. I was building a sandwich from the stump of a pork roast, cold bread, horseradish, mustard and mayonnaise, slivers of pickle. Children sauntered, biked and skateboarded by outside on their way home from school, children dressed in plaid skirts or charcoal-gray slacks, children in baggy cargo pants and bell-bottoms salvaged from thrift shops, children with processed hair, buzz cuts, bouffants, dreadlocks, multiple piercings. In the front room, off hall and telephone berth, NPR's *Talk of the Nation* beamed in from the greater world. As did this call.

"David?"

"I don't have much time. I just wanted to let you know that I'm all right, didn't want you worrying."

"Where are you?"

"Out in the world somewhere. That's what Buster Robinson and your other characters would say, right?" Someone spoke behind him. He covered the mouthpiece to respond, after a moment took his hand away. "Look, I'll be in touch soon, okay?"

"David—"

The connection went.

Most of an hour later, sandwich a scatter of crumbs on a chipped plate, half a bottle of California chardonnay sent after it, the fourth call came.

"'ew."

"No way this is good."

"Beg pardon?"

"Larson: you're using the phone. Scary, real scary. What's wrong?"

"It's 'ette. Paramedics are taking her to Baptist and I need to stay with 'Verne. Thought maybe you'd swing by there."

"The hospital, you mean."

"She's okay, but one of us needs to be there."

"What happened?"

"Oh, right. Okay. I'm on a job over in Metairie. Been there two, three months." Long enough to become forever, the only present, for Larson, something he had in common with Doo-Wop. "Gem of a house, kind you're not ever gonna see again."

"Okay."

"I've got my face two inches from the hardwood banister, going at it with the finest chise' I have, trying to reshape this thing, when Robert comes crabbing up the scaffo'd. Boy's got a ce'phone, on'y one who does—so we a'ways give out his number. For me, he says, and hands over the phone."

Officer McAllister calling. And this is . . . It's about your wife, I'm afraid. . . . First of all, let me assure you she's all right. . . .

A neighbor, old Miss Siler, placed the call. She'd been sitting out on her porch sipping at a toddy as she did most afternoons now she'd been retired from teaching after thirty-nine years ("More than one toddy, I suspect," McAllister said, "less than a dozen") and noticed a young man with a package under his arm stepping up onto Alouette's porch. He didn't ring the bell, which Miss Siler thought odd, but then he didn't do much of anything else either, so she lost interest. Next thing she knew, that young man was running off down the street like he had the very devil after him. Miss Siler looked back, up the street, across the yard, over the railing onto the porch, and there was Alouette, stretched out on the boards. She dialed 999, 919, finally got it right with 911. Officer McAllister responded.

Alouette was coming to as he arrived. She told him she'd heard someone on the gallery, boards creaking out there. She waited, and when no one came to the door, she opened it to look out. Thought she saw movement—someone hurrying around the bend? That was all she remembered. Presumably she'd stepped out onto the gallery. And someone *was* there. No sign of what the man had been carrying underarm. They did have one good impression of a footprint, McAllister said, looks like a heavy work shoe with waffle soles, where he vaulted over the banister, same banister she'd likely hit her head against.

"They're taking her out now, 'ew."

"Then I'm out of here too. On my way. I'll give you a call."

No one answered next door at Norm Marcus's house. I'd figured on snagging a ride in his cab, something I'd done before in similar situations, but that having failed, set out on foot, cutting through alleyways and across open lots, staggering in a broken run down Prytania, past St. Charles, along Napoleon Avenue to Baptist.

There in the ER I found Alouette standing beside a gurney simultaneously raging, enumerating inefficiencies of the system and demanding to be released. Five medical personnel stood facing her, hopelessly outnumbered. They hadn't a chance.

Everything's all right at home, I told her. Larson's with the kid. You okay?

"Fine—except that I've been abducted and now the aliens in their monotonous, unimaginative manner are preparing to perform medical experiments on me."

"The paramedics had to bring you in," one of the nurses said. "They're legally obliged to do so. We explained that to you."

"And I explained to *you* that I had no problem with that. They brought me. I came. Now my ride's here."

Doors swung open to admit a stretcher and two paramedics. One of them was reporting to the resident who'd met them out on the dock. The resident glanced over at me. One of her eyes drooped, the other looked wild.

". . . BP low but stable. Tourniquet's been in place just over twenty minutes. Out when we got there, but he's been conscious since. Alert and oriented. Stopped to help someone with car trouble, apparently. Had his hand under the hood when the driver decided to peel off. Took this one's arm, up to the elbow, with him. Probably still there under the hood."

"My ride's here," Alouette repeated, "and you have work to do."

Outside, we walked over to Claiborne. A cab pulled in to the curb to pick us up almost instantly. The driver, an elderly black man swaddled in layers against the cold, undershirt, plaid flannel shirt, checked sweater, sweatshirt zipped to his chin, nodded when I gave him our destination. He nodded again at the end, when I paid him. Never spoke.

"Thanks for saving me, Lew."

"Sure. Glad you don't mind."

"Am I really that difficult?"

"Yes."

She laughed. "Guess I could always claim I have no choice, it's in my genes."

Vehicles swarmed thickly about a windowless, bunkerlike store selling beer, wine and liquor at discount prices. Smoke wafted up from Henry's Soul Food and Pie Restaurant across the street. Four police cars sat outside.

"This wasn't the first time, Lew. The last couple of

letters, I thought I heard someone on the porch. I'd go out and find envelopes in the mailbox."

"You should have told me."

"I know."

Attaining Jefferson Avenue, the driver turned riverside. His tape of Sam Cooke done, he pushed in a new one, Barry White.

"At first I just didn't think it amounted to much. Later on, I guess my pride kicked in. I could take care of it myself. . . ."

"Fearless, like your mother."

"O yeah, that's me all right." When she looked up, I had a flash of her as a teenager. "I'm afraid all the time, Lew. Every day of my life, every hour and minute of it. Whatever I do, work, family, on some level it's just another way of keeping fear at bay. As a child, I used to wonder why I was so different, why others weren't afraid."

"Then you realized they were."

"Are they? I'm still not sure. Some are. You can see it in their eyes, the way they can't bear to be alone or in silence, in all the habits and hungers they'd swear to you are their passions. I remember how years ago, back when I was living with you that first time, you told me you didn't trust anyone who had no sense of humor. I think I feel the same way about people whose fear doesn't show."

"Maybe that's why you do the work you do."

She nodded. "It's why my mother did."

We sat quietly and I thought how proud I was of this young woman, of the life she'd made for herself. Maybe it *was* in the genes: she'd recapitulated her mother's transformation. Sitting beside her there with Barry's music flowing like honey, I was vividly aware of her youth, her vitality, of the warmth rising from her body. Of how much I loved her.

"You know what Hortense Callisher said?" she told me at the door. "*An apocalypse served in a very small cup*. That's what our lives are, Lew."

Then she went in to her family and I, after putting in the necessary appearance, offering up regrets, struck out homeward on foot. With each footfall my breath materialized before me, remained there a moment, and was gone. Only this light silk sportcoat for warmth. I had no notion what time it was. Growing late—I was safe with that. It's always growing late. Time enough, still, to meet my kinswoman Mrs. Molino?

27

I N my memory she's always there at the edge of things, sipping half cups of coffee, shuffling about in slippers: a small, ill-defined woman, face closed like a fist about—what? Pain? Her disaffection and disappointment with life, I suppose. Only in photographs, old photographs, did I ever see her smile. I don't know what made her go on. She had no passions that I know of. There was nothing she loved, nothing was ever as it should be, nothing was good enough. As years went on she faded ever further from life, her days held together by meager threads of routine. I recognize so much of her in myself, so much of myself in her.

28

S ELF-defense."

"What?"

"How I learned to cook. When I was a kid, we ate all this wonderful stuff, what people started calling soul food in the Sixties, corn bread, greens, pig tails, black-eyed peas, grits, salt meat. My parents were depression people, country folk. But then as urbanization kicked in full force, as the country grew more prosperous and all those wonderful progressive products hit the stores, little by little that wonderful food stopped showing up on the table. Canned peas and ground meat now. Biscuits out of cardboard tubes. You wouldn't think they could, but things got even worse when my mother went to work—she'd waited till I was in junior high. She was getting sicker by then, too, steadily falling away from the world. Food had never mattered to her. Now she'd bring home this stuff from the grocery store where she worked, TV dinners, mixes, prepackaged foods of all sorts, and that's what would show up on the table. When she did cook, she fried—a true Southerner. Or laid things out in a pressure cooker and turned them into something unrecognizable to sight *or* taste."

Mrs. Molino's hand, putting down her cup, continued across the table to my own. Nothing sexual in this for all her attractiveness, despite the physicality vibrating the very air around her. Simple human warmth, rather. She was one of those to whom connections came easy.

"I spent a lot of time later on, after I left home, reading cookbooks, just trying to puzzle my way through the basics. Wore a groove in kitchen tiles going back and forth from cookbooks to counter or stove."

Since we'd missed the reservation at Commander's, at my suggestion we'd gone instead to Jessie's, a neighborhood bar and grill of the sort that abounds here and almost nowhere else. There was a huge, wraparound old bar and only five or six small tables in the back for food service, but far more people came here to eat than to drink. The door rarely closed all the way: one customer caught it coming in as another, toting sacks, went out. Weekends, people lined up two or three deep at the bar having a Jax, bourbon or rum and coke as they waited. Jessie was a twig-thin albino with knobby joints, six-foot-four and 120 pounds tops, hair clipped short and so colorless it disappeared under lights, maroon eyes. His catfish po-boys, dressed with shredded lettuce, homemade pickle and his own remoulade, were the stuff of legend. I'd seen children in high chairs being fed pinches of these sandwiches by their parents. They'd probably grow up, move to Texas or Iowa, and need to be weaned. Decompressed, like deep-sea divers.

The coffee was almost as good. This, in a city that

takes its coffee seriously. Local legend had it that Jessie added a spoonful of graveyard dirt to each pot. Things like that made you consider how essentially pagan New Orleans could be. Citizens here still keep track of solstices, favor Halloween and All Saints' Day over Christmas.

"You and Deborah've been together awhile."

I nodded.

"Is this it, do you think?"

"I suspect so. She's never been one to make arbitrary or tentative moves."

"Then I'm sorry, Lewis."

I was about to say more when Don stepped through the doorway, glanced around, and walked towards us, followed in short order by Rick Garces.

"I'm going to assume you're looking for me, and didn't just stop by for a catfish fix."

"Nah. Roast beef's better, anyway."

"So how'd you find me?"

"You mentioned you were meeting with Dr. Guidry—"

I was fairly certain I hadn't, but let it pass.

"—so I swung by. Mrs. Molino here—"

"Catherine: Don Walsh, Rick Garces. Both old friends."

"—left her destination with the housekeeper, in case she was needed."

"Good to see you, Rick." We shook hands. "Been some time. Why do I remember you as smaller?"

"Probably because I was. And it's all your fault. You took me to that Cuban restaurant the first time, now I can't stay out of there. José has a Cuban coffee working, sandwich soaking up grease on the grill, before I'm through the door. Then afterwards the damn fool brings me flan on the house. And I'm damn fool enough to eat it."

As we spoke, Catherine had discreetly gone off

and borrowed chairs for them both from other tables. Embarrassed, as much from not noticing as from her ministry, they sat.

"And what does Eugene think of that?" I asked. Eugene had enlarged, cropped and framed my favorite photo of LaVerne, a snapshot Rick took just before she died, when she'd stuck her head in his door at the Foucher's Women Shelter where they both worked to ask Rick about a client.

"More of you to love, is what he says."

"Good man."

"You bet he is."

I went back to the window behind the bar to tell Jessie we needed four coffees when he had the chance. Steam from the grill wreathed his face. "Ever think about getting some help in here?"

"You volunteering?"

"I could get the coffees."

"You do that. And while you're at it, see who else needs a refill. Pot must be scraping bottom 'long about now too, so maybe you could pour in some water, drop in a filter. Then fill the sucker up—to the top—with French Market."

"Sure, just tell me where you keep the dirt."

"Come again?"

"Forget it."

I did what he asked, pulled a battered ancient Coke tray out from under the counter and used it to carry four cups of fresh coffee back to our table. Santa with a squat bottle tilted into his beard, sixty dollars or more at any flea market. Catherine, Don and Rick were in spirited conversation.

"You can set up systems to provide basic needs. Service, employment, housing. No problem there. But what do you do about incentive? Much as we'd like it to, Maslow's hierarchy doesn't just kick in like an afterburner."

"Same dilemma as at the heart of socialist and communist forms of government."

"Right."

"Whereas capitalism tends inevitably to monopolies and centralization of wealth," Don said.

I stared at him.

He shrugged. "Lots of spare time these days. I've been reading some."

"Because motivation has to come from within," Catherine said.

"Does it? There's no greater motivator, for some, than wealth accumulation. Status. Both of those are external counters. Meanwhile, what seems an ever-growing percentage of our population *has* no motivation."

I sat listening, watching the steady exchange of customers through the door. When finally the tiniest hairline of a break opened in the conversation, I said, "God I hope the bell rings soon."

"Anyone know who this man's with?" Rick asked.

"So what are you guys doing here?"

Don's eyes met mine. Again I thought: lands and grooves of my own life, my own years, on someone else's face. "Rick and I were having lunch last week—"

"At Casa Verde."

"Right."

"Sandwich, coffee."

"Three coffees, maybe four."

"Four coffees?"

"Hey. Small cups."

"And flan," Rick said.

"Of course."

"He wanted to know how you and Alouette were doing, how the baby was. Somewhere along the way—"

"Third napkin, as I recall."

"*Good* grease."

"Absolutely."

"—I mentioned the letters she's been getting."

"He also mentioned the unexpected contact you'd had with Alouette's father. I went home and the more I thought about that, the odder it seemed to me. What did he want?"

"To find someone, he said."

"But then he didn't want that anymore. And why you? With his means, he could hire a battery of folks to do a search."

"Even people who actually find who they're looking for," Don put in.

"Very funny. I assumed it was his roundabout way of trying to make contact with Alouette."

"Maybe . . ."

Jessie materialized beside the table, carrying a platter. Enough food on there to feed everyone in the Desire projects.

"We've gone to finger-food heaven," Catherine said.

"Anyone works here gets fed free. Gator tails," pointing. "Catfish. Meatballs in my own marinara. Pickles—I make them, too. Slices of chicken breast marinated in barbeque sauce and grilled."

"Good, Jessie," I said. "This makes an awful lot of sense. I put in six minutes, tops, helping out, and that mainly because we need coffee, so you spend twice that putting this platter together."

He shrugged and went back to his kitchen, only place he ever felt right.

"Have to admit it's one hell of a coincidence," Garces went on. "Dickensian. But life's never story-shaped. I kept thinking: Whatever's being said here, it's not what's being said."

There were, along with gator tails, catfish, meatballs, chicken and sliced vegetables, small pots of ranch dressing, mustard with hot peppers chopped into it, a dish of fresh cilantro and mint. We all tucked in. Don went off towards the kitchen to confer with Jessie, then to the bar, and brought back beers.

"Now *you* work here," I said, "and he's gonna bring more."

"No end to it."

"We'll never get out of here."

"I go home and start poking about, using this loose network that's developed over the years."

"One you used to find Alouette."

"The same. Social workers like myself, psychiatric nurses, aides, people from support groups, family members, ex-patients. Not too many of those at first. Lots more these past few years. Whole thing's fishing, drop in tackle and flies, hope for strikes. Nothing jumps right out, maybe for a while, maybe never. But that's what I do.

"Then one night I can't get to sleep, finally give up on fighting the bedclothes—it's so bad that ditties from *Carmen* and old Randy Newman songs are running loose in my head, rattling around in there like marbles. And the bedclothes are definitely winning, they've pinned me eight times out of ten. So after an hour of watching bad movies on TV, women warriors whose acting consists of contorting their mouths, male leads so stupid you wonder how they ever managed to find the dryer and hair spray, I settled down in front of the computer and tossed out a few new lines. Most of them just went spinning on out and didn't catch anywhere, as usual. But one or two snagged, got responses that brought up new queries, suggested some direction or flight path I hadn't thought of before. I started feeling my way carefully, like crossing a muddy field on stepping-stones. Around four that morning I found myself talking to a bus driver who'd spent nineteen months in a clinic up near Fort Worth. Bus driver now, but back before the breakdown he'd been a pilot. Not only was his insurance good but his family had money, so he wound up there, one of those got-it-covered private asylums, instead of across the river at Mandeville.

"His name's Tony Sinclair. Once he started getting better, he asked if there was anything he could do to help out. Always been a hard worker and couldn't stand the inactivity anymore, feeling so useless, he told me. So he started out doing this and that, not much of anything at all at first, really. Reading to other patients, walking with them out on the grounds, helping them get dressed or write letters home, that kind of thing. But gradually he took on more and more. Before long he'd worked his way into the back wards and was helping take care of the really sick ones. Got to know some of them pretty well, that last year."

A face appeared in the window beside us, in the scant space left at one edge of the ancient lettering, J E S S   E ' S, above placards pitching gospel shows and revivals. The man's breath fogged the glass, which partially cleared then fogged again with another breath and another, so that, frost building by increments, bit by bit his face disappeared. He wore three or four shirts, a hunter's cap with earflaps, shiny wool trousers held up by suspenders, one side of which had been replaced by hemp twine.

"Sinclair's the kind of guy you instinctively trust and want to talk to. He wasn't, no way I'd be up hitting keys back and forth to him at four or five in the morning."

"People like that make good investigators," Don said.

"They make great social workers and therapists, too. Only problem is, they tend to burn out. . . . Anyhow, some of these guys on back wards started talking to him, guys who hadn't said anything to anyone, some of them, for years. Not that there's any kind of dialogue or conversation going on, understand. But things would just jump out there from time to time.

"Early one morning Sinclair's attending this young man, he's in his thirties, name given as Danny Eskew. White skin, straight dark hair, negroid features. According to records he's not only mentally ill—schizophrenia—but also severely retarded. Anoxic insult, they figured. Sinclair's not so sure. He's noticed Eskew's eyes following him around the room, wondering who he is maybe, what he's doing here. Blinds are open, Sinclair's shaving him, and just as he lifts the razor, a shaft of sunlight catches on it, gets thrown, blindingly, up onto the wall.

"'Sharp,' Eskew blurts out as his eyes find it.

"'Razor's too sharp?' Maybe he was hurting him.

"'Light.'

"He waited, but that was it. Week or so later, he was reading to this guy, *The Count of Monte Cristo*, only thing he could find in the hospital library that looked interesting, when Eskew spoke up again.

"'No . . . story,' he said.

"'What do you mean?' Then: 'Danny?'

"A long time went by, Sinclair said, before Eskew said anymore. Then he said: 'Me.'

"Hackles rose when I heard that. Hair standing up on my neck, what the Russians call chicken skin. Sinclair'd had much the same response, which is why he passed it along to me. That was it, though: the last thing he ever heard from Danny Eskew. 'Maybe I'm reading too much into it. Maybe I've been doing that all along,' he said.

"I didn't think so. But it was definitely time for me to surface, flip things over to official sites. So I logged on and started raking records for psychiatric facilities and private clinics in or around Fort Worth. Dredged up lots of nothing at first—not that I expected much else. I called in to work to let them know I'd be late, might not even make it at all, and kept going."

"But you knew where he, this Sinclair, was."

"Which helped not much at all. Records from facilities like that are locked down tight. They call themselves private and they damn well mean to stay that way. That's a large part of their appeal, and what clients pay for.

"So what I'm doing is backtracking. Looking for ghosts, echoes, footprints on the beach. Records from local hospitals, say, from years back. Parkland, John Peter Smith. Those are public records and accessible—at least partially. Same with social services like Child Welfare, MHMR. Or schools, whose counselors and nurses often note what others fail to.

"Sometimes you only have to snag one loose end, a single thread. I found my strand a little after ten this morning and started worrying at it, hopscotching off a couple of Dallas-area hospital admissions. The second admission carried a court date—court's held right there in MDC, just up Harry Hines from Parkland—but it got canceled for no apparent reason, and at the last moment. We're talking pro forma here, cookie-cutter. Cancellations like that just do *not* happen.

"But at that point, whatever weirdness is going on, I've got a fix on him. He's in the system. Lawyers and conservators can tuck him away, but they can't hide him. Another hour or so on the phone, I've got a rough history."

"Lawyers and conservators," I said.

"Mm-hm."

Our Gentleman of the Half Suspenders was back at the window. Holding up a burger proudly, he proceeded to eat it for us. Grease worked its way along his whiskery chin; catsup, mustard and saliva splattered onto the glass. Finished, he wiped hands on wool pants and blew us a kiss.

"Plan on seeing Dr. Guidry anytime soon?"

"Why?"

Don and Rick exchanged glances.

"When you do, you might ask about Danny Eskew."

"Yeah," Don said. "Ask him how his son's doing."

29

L ET me assure you, Mr. Griffin, there's absolutely no way, no way at all . . . this young man . . . could be involved."

This young man.

"Dr. Guidry first learned of his existence," Catherine said after a moment, "when Danny was fifteen, and then only because the boy had come onto such trouble. The mother was at wit's end, with nowhere else to turn."

"And she is . . . ?"

"A former secretary."

Guidry's face was turned towards the window. He could have been remembering this woman he'd briefly loved so long ago. Or watching dark angels of regret gather out on the schoolyard.

"He's never felt any connection or kinship to the boy. Why should he? But he has, from the moment he learned of the boy's existence, taken full responsibility for his care."

"Removing all authority from the mother—"

"At her express request, yes."

"And committing his son for life."

"What else was he to do, Lewis? The boy is incapacitated, profoundly ill. This isn't some prime-time TV show where he's going to snap out of it in the last five minutes and head over to the mall on a shopping spree."

"Yet he seems to have been normal up till what—fourteen, fifteen?"

"That's often when mental illness begins to manifest itself, especially schizophrenia."

"No indication of deficiency, retardation."

"At that point, no." Giving me her full attention, she also managed somehow to keep an eye on Guidry, whose head again had lowered onto his chest, coaxing forth soft snores.

"Danny's first serious hospitalization was in a satellite clinic in Oak Cliff, one of a dozen or more communities thronging around Dallas to make up the Metroplex. Six weeks, by court order. Fifth week, he took the meds he'd been hoarding all that time, fifty, sixty pills, maybe more. They didn't find him till morning, just after seven, when an orderly went through bouncing beds and calling out. His head lay in a pool of vomit. Respirations were shallow, down to six or so, barely visible. The orderly screamed for help and started mouth-to-mouth. Danny came back, but he'd been down a while. His brain had gone too long without adequate oxygen. It was shortly after that that the boy's mother got in touch with Dr. Guidry."

"Did Guidry visit? Actually see Danny face-to-face?"

"Once. He never spoke of it afterwards."

"So the boy's care fell to others."

"To the same group of lawyers and advisors who oversee all his financial affairs, yes."

"Then he would have received regular reports."

"He did."

"Did he read them?"

"I can't say. They were passed along to him."

"Up the food chain. By?"

"Myself, for some years now. Others before I came."

"Secretaries, you mean. Personal assistants."

"Yes."

We'd been speaking as though he were no longer in the room, which, in a sense, he wasn't. But now Guidry's head rose. He turned his gaze to us, eyes clear.

"I can say, Mr. Griffin." He grimaced as pain thrust and withdrew. "I read every word, many times over. If words could be used up, those would have been empty shells, nothing more. Hundreds upon hundreds of them. Empty shells."

I watched as something else, something in its own way as substantial as the pain, arrived.

"One summer, long ago, my parents rented a cabin up in Arkansas, a place called Maddox Bay. Near your homeland, I believe. Beautiful country."

"Others think so. I could never see it."

"Often one doesn't. . . . Generally we vacationed on Grand Isle, where my grandparents owned a cabin, or over in Biloxi. One of my earliest memories is of Biloxi, green trees and grass, then a low wall and nothing else but sand to water's edge—sand they had to ship in truckload by truckload from somewhere else, though of course I didn't know that at the time. They had two or three of these squat, blocky, ugly things called Ducks, aquatic landing vehicles left over from the war, and they'd take tourists for rides in them.

"Nothing like that on Maddox Bay, though. Nothing for tourists. Just a lot of thrown-together shacks, porches and patios tacked onto cheap aluminum trailers set up on blocks. Boats with outboard motors the size of oil drums coursed in and out from rough docks or slid directly down muddy banks into scummy water. I loved the way they'd slow, cut back to almost nothing, whenever they passed other boats with people fishing, then rev back up. Fishermen cleaned their catch on the bank, tossing scales, fins, heads and intestines back in the water.

"One late afternoon I came walking out of the woods, bank neither dull, dirt nor mud here but heaped with seashells, hundreds of them, thousands, that glinted powerfully in late sunlight, crunching as I walked into them. They appeared whole at first, but when I bent to pick one up and looked closely, not much was left: only the overall form, a patchwork of narrow bridges between round holes.

"Buttons, my father explained when I told him of my discovery. They'd punched out holes in all those shells to make buttons, then dumped them there, in mounds."

His eyes strayed again to the window, back to us.

"There was a point to all this. Really there was."

"You need to rest now," Catherine said.

"You're right, my dear. One of many things I need. Most of which I'll never have."

She took him off to bed and, twenty minutes later, returned, sinking down beside me on the steel-gray leather couch.

"I had to let him tell you, Lewis. It wasn't my place to do so."

"I understand."

For a time then, we sat without speaking.

"I'm so tired. I can't even begin to imagine how *he* must feel."

"Someday you have to tell me how you came to be here, doing this," I said.

"Does it really seem that strange to you?"

"Ever the more, as I get to know you."

"Then someday I will." Her head rested against

my shoulder. "I've aways been a sucker for men who say ever the more."

Moments later, she was asleep.

"I'm faxing through a list of employees from that period. To Assistant Superintendent Santos at NOPD, right?"

"Right." My own fax hadn't worked in years. Don suggested Santos, who agreed over the phone with a verbal shrug.

"This is all . . . unorthodox, Mr. Griffin."

"I appreciate that, Dr. Ball. And I thank you for your help."

"I do have assurances from my colleague Richard Garces and from Captain Don Walsh—"

Captain Emeritus, I'd have to start calling him.

"—both of whom vouch for you personally, and for the legitimacy of your request. They explained what was going on here. God knows women in our society are prey to enough, without this sort of thing. I can only hope the information will help you."

"Yes, sir. I'm sure it will."

"The list should at any rate be with Officer Santos now. I've alerted my secretary, Miss Eddington—"

For a moment I thought he said Errington.

"—that you may call back. She should be able to help you with any further information or assistance you need."

"Once again, doctor, thank you."

The line stayed open.

"Is there anything else?"

"Look, I know this is a long shot. You couldn't possibly be the same Lewis Griffin who wrote *Skull Meat* and *The Old Man*, right?"

"Right."

"Right you couldn't?"

"Right I am."

"My God. I have a first edition of *Skull Meat*."

"Not many of those around these days."

"Tell me about it. Took me years to find one. And I gave up a few dinners for it."

"The thing sold for sixty cents."

"Exactly. Look, there's no reason you'd remember me . . ."

I waited.

"I did my psychiatric residency at Mandeville. Ears that stuck out like jug handles, and I was greener than green, only the vaguest idea what I was doing or even what I was supposed to be doing—not that I realized it at the time. That was, I don't know, forty years ago? Some time well into the Sixties, anyway. I took care of you, Mr. Griffin. You were my patient."

"Dr. Ball. . . . I remember. You looked like a kid on his paper route."

"I *was* a kid."

"You came to the ward, had to be past midnight. They came and got me out of the dorm. You'd been off for the weekend, and whoever covered for you had cut meds without telling me. I thought it was all coming back on me. You heard about it when the other doctor reported off and were worried."

"I was trying to cover my ass."

"That's not what I saw in your face. What I saw there was kindness—something I didn't see often around those parts."

Hornets hung buzzing in the line as neither of us spoke.

"The parts haven't changed."

"Then maybe we have, at least."

"We hope."

Half an hour later I'd worked my way a few inches into a bottle of Scotch and had the TV on, clicking back and forth from news reports to the "reality shows" that had become so popular—middle-class men and women plucked from comfortable lives and inserted where they had no business being, prisons, ghettos, deserted islands, strolling about beneath the umbrella of hidden cameras—unable finally to see much difference, all of it a blur. The news as presented seemed to me no less fictive or contrived than the situations of these shows. I'd been cast into some latter-day vortex, Poe's maelstrom.

In the storm of information around us, events are reported as they occur. Breathlessly we're rushed from one crisis or catastrophe to another. Broomstraws of truth get driven, quivering like arrows, into the sides of houses, barns, telephone poles. Cows appear bellowing on roofs. Tension mounts and mounts but there's never resolution. Cameras, reporters and commentators move on to the next big thing, the latest country invaded or fallen to military coup, the newest political scandal, this week's hot actor or teenage music sensation. We're caught in an endless loop, there's no way out.

"I woke you."

"Well . . . yes. It *is* the middle of the night."

The phone was a dead, cold thing in my hand. Without sound the TV went on spilling errant light, images and icons into the room. I looked at the clock. Just past three. Time of night when ancients thought the soul drifted farthest from the body and might be harvested.

"I'm sorry, Catherine."

I listened as her breathing changed.

"Is something wrong?"

"No. I came home, had a few drinks—"

"I can tell that."

"—but couldn't sleep." Guidry's Proustian fugues

had taken root in me. My mind became a city dump, trucks pulling in every five minutes, barrels of refuse tumbling over one another, vermin swarming. "I started off thinking about apartments I've lived in. Next it was bits and pieces of books."

"Yours?"

"And others'. Before long, I'd moved on to remembering old friends. And after that I was all over the place. Thinking about my first trumpet, of all things. My parents got it off some friend they said had played with the territory bands back in the Forties. Looked to be made out of pot metal and kept falling apart at the struts, it'd just come open like a book in the middle of songs. Or a yellow nylon shirt I had as a kid. You could see right through it, and the thing was light as a scarf, light as breath itself. For a week or two that was the coolest thing I'd ever seen, coolest thing I'd ever owned.

"Then I remembered a school project, seventh grade, maybe. We were reading *Great Expectations* and had to do something to 'illustrate or dramatize' Dickens's imagination. But it wasn't Dickens's imagination that interested me, and I went right to the heart of what did. In my father's workshop I built a small platform, like a stage set, divided in half. One side showed things the way Miss Havisham saw them: the wedding veil, the cake and so on. And the other half showed what it was all really like. Cobwebs, the rotted gown. At the time I couldn't have had any idea that I was defining a vital space for myself, recognizing that a kind of zone or crawl space existed between those two worlds."

"I see. And this is what you called to tell me at three o'clock in the morning, Lewis?"

"No."

"What, then?"

"I'm not sure. . . . I think I may have called to tell you that I've lived there ever since."

Her laugh was as light and airy, as much a miracle, as my nylon shirt.

"Of course you have."

30

A T first I couldn't think why I knew the place, then remembered: the ex-ranger back at the pigeon hunters' apartment.

Hoppin Jon's. From outside it looked like a cement bunker. Inside, it was one room the size of a dance hall or bowling alley. At the far end, a low brick wall set off kitchen area and cooks; a round bar stood dead center. Otherwise the floor space was broken only by homemade tables of whitewashed wood, some of them small, others picnic-size, pushed about the floor into casual combinations and collisions. Even now, at breakfast, the place smelled, as so many New Orleans restaurants do, of fried shrimp.

Three dozen or so patrons sat, stood or milled about. Looked a little like a prison yard during an eclipse. Most of them had plates of food, all of them had drinks. The drinks came in what appeared to be honest-to-God jelly glasses. Terence Braly was at a communal table halfway in. Santos had remained behind at the door as we entered; now he leaned easily against the wall, looking around with no expression on his face. Don had kept moving to take position in the rear, near bathrooms and whatever exit they or the kitchen might offer. When I sat down by him, our boy's friends all found their feet and went away. Most of them no doubt saw me come in with Santos and Don and figured us all for cops. The others just had feelers out—kind of work they did, they developed feelers—and knew when to (as Chandler said) be missing.

"E*xcuse* me," he said. White, five-six or right around there, dark hair with tight curls. Pushing thirty but hanging back in the breezeway. He still had on his hospital uniform. He'd unzipped the green top. A ribbed undershirt showed beneath; his employee badge, alligator-clipped to the collar, flapped under-arm. White pants bore a permanent crease you could use to slice bagels. Shoes white too, Reeboks, recently polished but with traces of grime and possibly dry blood around eyelets and seams. "Do you *mind*?"

Smiling, I said nothing, and moved still closer to him. Sensed, as though they were my own, heartbeat and respirations increasing.

"I know you?"

"Nope." I reached over and picked up his glass. Took, as my old friend O'Carolan and several centuries of traditional singers might say, a healthy dram. Put the glass back exactly where it had been, in the ring it came out of. "Okay, one question down, nine to go."

"Man," he said, drawing the *n* out to its breaking point, "that's my fucking drink. You wanta get out of my face here?"

"No. Eight."

He took a long breath. Maybe a change of tactic was in order. "Look, man, whatever your thing is, can we get into it some other time? Been a long night, I'm just not up to this."

"Those old folks do take their toll, don't they?"

He braced himself from glancing at me and instead looked off, something he'd seen tough guys do in movies. Eyes stayed there in the middle distance when he spoke.

"Man, whoever you are, I don't have anything you need, you know? And what I do have, you don't want."

But he was crimping. Part of the reason he did the work he did and hung on to it was that it allowed him a control wholly absent from the rest of his life. Whatever tension or danger he faced, whatever bad guys, the weight of authority bulked behind him, the deliverance of routine bore him up. Now he found himself face-to-face with one of those bad guys outside the palace grounds, no one else around, rules gone south.

I put my hand over his, joints bulky as pecans beneath my palm, and bore down. When he tried to pull away, for a moment I bore down still harder, then let him withdraw.

"Maybe I could buy you a drink," I said. "Several drinks."

Cage door left open, free at last, free at last, his eyes came back to me.

"Okay. Tha'd be all right."

"Canadian Club and 7-Up, right?"

"Sweet. . . . Don't worry, man. I saw your posse, I ain't going nowhere. They step back long enough to let me have a piss, you think?"

"Absolutely. Nod to Cerberus as you go by, guy in the yellow shirt. Best keep your distance, though. He recently got shot. It's made him edgy."

"I hear you." He started off towards the back as Don and I exchanged glances. I snagged a CC-and-7 and a brandy at the bar, waited for Terence back at the table.

"Alouette says hello," I told him, pushing the drink his way.

He picked it up and took a long pull. "Damn that's good. Guess I'm screwed, huh?"

"Sure looks that way."

"So how'd you find me?"

"Does it matter?"

He shrugged.

We'd flagged his name, along with others, on the list of employees sent us by Dr. Ball. He'd been an orderly at the psychiatric facility in Fort Worth, assigned for the most part (a call to Dr. Ball's Miss Eddington disclosed) to back wards, when Tony Sinclair was there, and left shortly thereafter. Over the next several years, as Rick was able to track, his name showed up on rosters at half a dozen or more facilities in Louisiana, Alabama and Texas. Now he worked at a geriatric hospital here in the city. Most human resources records are elliptical, Rick said, and in a kind of code, but it isn't a hard code to read, and what it comes down to is that Terence had started getting too close to his patients, identifying with them, claiming communication and levels of interaction no one else ever witnessed.

"I didn't mean to hurt anyone."

"I'm willing to believe that."

I'd never drunk Courvoisier from a jelly glass before. Aroma and taste of the brandy coloring my world, smoothing it, pulling things together as it always does, I told him who I was. Told him about LaVerne and our life together, how I'd gone looking for Alouette and found her up in Mississippi with her baby. How after the baby died, I brought her home. How she'd stayed around a while, left, and years later returned.

"She was on the streets, then."

I nodded. "You didn't know much about her."

"No. I didn't." He looked off again, nothing histrionic about it this time, and for some moments grew silent. "I thought I was helping. I was trying to."

I got us new drinks at the bar. Terence sampled his and said, "I was on the street myself till I was nineteen, twenty. Starting when I was, I don't know, ten? eleven?"

"What happened to your parents?"

He shrugged. "They died, maybe. Or I ran off. I don't remember much of anything before being on the streets, really. Seems like I was always out there. I learned everything I know from people I met—how to get along, how to find food, where to sleep. I'd watch them, copy what they did. Got older, I started wondering if there *was* a me somewhere in there. Maybe I was just this pasteup, this artificial thing. A bad copy, you know?"

All signs being that our boy wasn't going to bolt or attack, Don and Santos came in from the field.

"You gonna be okay here, Griffin?" Santos said.

I nodded.

"Then I better get back to the work the citizens pay me for."

"I'm grabbing breakfast. You want anything, Lew?" Don asked. He started off.

"Captain . . ." Santos said.

"Yeah?"

"Dinner, man. That rain check you've been holding has to be faded out by now. My wife's a patient woman, but you put it off much longer she's likely to turn up at your door. One thing you don't want's a pissed-off Cuban coming round. I ever tell you about the time her father ran into Lee Harvey Oswald on the street handing out communist pamphlets?"

"I'll check with Jeanette, give you a call."

Santos nodded to Don, then to me. He headed for the door, Red Sea of patrons parting before him.

"Every few months," Terence went on, "I'd get scooped up off the streets and sent to some holding center, or farmed out to foster homes. I'd escape—

one time, I crawled out through holes knocked in old walls to make room for air-conditioning, another time I hid in barrels of garbage—or more often I'd just walk away.

"Then late one afternoon I ran smack into a wall I couldn't get through or around. Don't think I didn't try. But instead of packing me off upstate or exiling me to some godawful suburb, Judge Branning took me home with him. The house was filled with kids, three or four of them his own (I was never sure how many or which), the rest a mixture of neighborhood kids, other kids hooked up with one or the other for schoolwork or projects, and kids who'd come through his court and still dropped by from time to time.

"I wasn't a kid, of course, and I made sure they all knew that. Way I walked, talked, way I kept myself apart from the rest. I'd been on my own a long time. Late that night, the judge found me out on the porch. Everyone else was either gone or in bed. I was sitting there with my feet hanging off. He'd had a few drinks by then—Judge loved his bourbon—and his speech was a little slurred.

"'Don't do what most of us do, son,' he said. 'Don't get along towards the end of your life, look around you, and realize you've wasted it.'

"That's all he said. We sat there, him on the big swing, me on the floor by the edge. A shooting star sliced through the sky. Cars and trucks passed by on the street, heavier traffic out on the interstate. 'How you figure I can get 'round that?' I asked him. 'I been thinkin' on it,' he said. 'I still am.'

"Next morning he took me down to the local hospital. Not to the employment office, but right on into the hospital administrator's. 'Got a good man here,' he said after he'd introduced us, 'who needs good work.' Administrator looked me over. 'Well, I don't know about good,' he said, 'but we sure enough got *hard*

220 ◆ JAMES SALLIS

work needs doing. Good might come later.' Judge looked over at me: 'What you think?' 'I reckon that should do for now,' I told them."

Don rejoined us bearing a plate of eggs, sausage, home fries and toast aswim in grease.

"Yum."

"Get your own."

"One way or another," Terence said, "I been at it ever since. Felt like I was doing something that mattered, you know? Not just moving papers around, trying to sell people something they don't need."

I nodded.

"Funny thing can happen to people who work health care for a long time. I don't know, maybe they just see too much, reach some kind of limit. Or have to protect themselves. But they lose sight of what it's all about, stop feeling anything for those they're taking care of. Not hard to see how that might happen, but with me it was just the opposite. More time I spent doing the work, the more I felt for those I was caring for, the more I wanted to do for them. Taking care of their basic needs, medical needs, just being there, wasn't enough anymore."

"Danny Eskew, for instance."

"Right. You know what it's like to be rejected by your family, cast off like old clothing, furniture that clashes with new curtains? He was the man in the iron mask, shut away for life from everything human. Sitting there unable to feed himself, messing himself as often as not, staring at walls and waiting—with nothing to wait for. Meanwhile there's this family elsewhere, this half-sister his father absolutely adores. Danny knew all that. How do you think it made him feel?"

"The doctors taking care of him say there's no way he could have known."

"Psychiatrists . . ."

"And even if he did know, there's no way he could have communicated it."

"Not to them. But I think I knew the first time I walked into his room. It's like that sometimes. You walk close enough to them, their soul leaps into your own. It's an electric arc. Blue, and all but blinding—you can almost smell it afterwards. Like a welder's torch."

"You guys want another drink?" Don asked.

"No. No, I don't think so. But thanks, man."

I shook my head.

"Okay. So you identified with Danny Eskew. I can understand that. What I'm not clear on is how you get from there to stalking Alouette."

"No, no. That's not it, not at all, I don't identify with Danny. This has nothing to do with me. Stalking her? God, no. I'm only trying to help. The girl doesn't know about her brother, doesn't even know he exists. She should. And he's stranded, marooned, all alone. I'm just a channel, a conduit, from Danny to his sister. Through me he's reaching out, speaking to her."

"There on the porch, for instance?"

"I'm sorry about that. I didn't think she was home. When I heard her coming out, I panicked—started to run, then in my confusion turned around and ran right into her. I'm glad she wasn't hurt."

"Where'd William Blake come from?" Don said suddenly. You'd have sworn he hadn't been paying the least attention.

"Another patient of mine. Old soul, he called himself. Always going on about Madame Blavatsky, Nostradamus, Native Americans. Had a book about Blake on top of a stack of them in his room. I picked it up one morning and it fell open to this picture of a painting, some kind of monster walking across a wooden floor, with curtains right by him so that it looks like he's on a stage. The book was there for me to find. Instantly I realized that I'd known that painting forever, though I'd never seen it before. Since then I've read everything by and about Blake there is. . . . Maybe I *will* have that drink.

"Blake talked to angels, you know," he said when Don came back with our drinks.

"Yeah. Yeah, I heard that. You?"

Terence nodded. "They don't answer very often, though."

31

As we stood by the front door saying final things that morning, a youngish man in watch cap and sweater had come to the window outside. In the moment before the frost of his breath obscured it, his face showed, and when the frost cleared, he was gone. For that moment I could have sworn it was my son's face pressed there against the glass, looking in.

Two hours later, at home trying to piece back together with coffee what brandy had torn down, I was still remembering that face outside when the phone rang.

"Lewis, haven't seen you down to the park of late."

"Lester. How are you?"

"Fit, thank you. Yourself?"

"I'm good. . . . The boy's okay?"

"Never better. That boy and Mr. Blue are inseparable. Just sit there looking out the window for hours at a time, the both of them content as can be. Boy gets a bath, Mr. Blue has to be in there too. I fix the boy lunch, I got to fix somethin' for Mr. Blue. Beats all I've seen. That was a good thing you did, Lewis."

"I'm glad it worked out."

"You ought to get on down to the park soon and have you a look. Bring along a good coat though, that wind'll slice meat right off your bones. And you won't believe it when you see it. Pigeons came sweeping back in all at the same time, like they knew. Like they were coming home. That park's a little corner of my heart's country—you know that. Seeing those birds again did my heart some righteous good."

"Tell the boy I said hello?"

"I'll surely do that. And will I be seeing you?"

"Soon. I promise."

Hanging up, I thought for a moment how lonely Lester must be. How lonely we all are, all of us like Ulysses just trying to find our way home. And I thought about my son. Maybe there is something to this notion of karma. Maybe the good things we do—Guidry's sponsorship of the school, Alouette's community work, even Terence Braly's efforts in their own way—maybe somehow these can make up for all the rest.

I'd gone out to the kitchen to pour the rest of the coffee down the sink, a healthy dram or two of Scotch into my cup, when the phone rang again. Carried cup towards the hall and dipped into it as I lifted the phone. Cast down your bucket where you are, as Booker T. Washington advised us.

"Good morning, Lew. Hope I didn't wake you."

"Not at all. Up and working."

A pause, then: "Working?"

I filled her in on the past few days, Alouette, Terence Braly, these latest brambles and snags. "How are you?"

"Fine, just fine. . . . We opened last night. It went well. Extraordinarily well, I think. . . . I hoped you might be there."

"I'm sorry."

"That's okay. I didn't think you would, I just hoped." She was quiet a moment. "Am I never going to see you again, Lew? I'd hate that. I'm not sure I could stand it."

"You'll see me."

"Good."

Doors, I thought. Their hearts do business like their doors. Apollinaire. LaVerne telling me how as a child she'd look out the back of train windows at all the people and places she passed, these lives she'd never see again, every passage a chain of good-byes. Alouette at the door when I'd ferried her home from the hospital: Our lives are an apocalypse served in a very small cup.

"I'm glad to hear things went well."

"The place was packed, Lew. Packed. I couldn't believe it. Blue-haired little old ladies, students lugging backpacks, even a couple of families with kids in strollers. White-faced young women in all black, bangs, clunky shoes. Others in evening dresses complete with mouth-watering show of thigh and breast. Most of one whole row was all Willie's friends. Remember Willie? I told you about him."

"Rap version of Greek choruses."

"That's the one. Calls himself Bad Dog Number Fifteen—which is how he insisted we list him on the program. And these guys, his posse he calls them, were having more fun than anyone else. Slumped down in seats with their big-legged droopy pants and oversize shirts, talking low among themselves. Willie's a talent, Lew. A natural who came out of nowhere. He gave me a copy of this play he wrote, *British Knights*. It's so good that after I read it I wanted to just go off somewhere and cry. I knew I could never write anything like that."

Moments pulled themselves like discarded newspapers across the floor towards sunlight.

"I've been meaning to tell you this, Lew. When I was researching early theatre, I found an article on what seems to be the first real civilization. Mesopotamia, on the banks of the Tigris and Euphrates, 2500 B.C. The Sumerians kept extensive records, etched them in a script they'd devised onto damp clay tablets which were then baked. Eventually, like all others, their civilization declined. The great libraries and record houses where they stored these tablets, these documents of what they'd been personally and collectively, of how they'd lived their lives and the *more* they'd envisioned—all this fell into ruin or burned to the ground. Walls crumbled back to stone, but the tablets remained. Fires that consumed libraries and whole cities simply turned the clay tablets brick-red, baked them to a new durability."

"The city falls, the pillars stay." Apollinaire again. Or stretching further back: All Pergamum is covered with thorn bushes, even its ruins have perished.

"I knew you'd like it."

"That I'd steal it, you mean. And I will, first chance I get."

She laughed. "I've got to go, Lew. The production's been extended, it's on through the end of the month, Tuesdays through Saturdays. Maybe longer, who knows? And maybe you'll come some night." Getting no response, she said, "I miss you."

Then I stood with the phone's black anvil in my hand, dial tone in my ear.

That morning, as we stood outside Hoppin Jon's, me looking around to see if by any chance I could spot the youngish man who'd just been looking in, Don and I had parted.

"I know, I know. You'll walk. Damn, I forgot to lock the thing again." He pulled the door open and stood there in the notch. "Few more years, we're both in those motorized wheelchairs, you'll probably still cut out on your own. Hitch a ride behind a garbage truck, way kids do on bikes."

"Surely it won't come to that."

It didn't.

Shaking his head and grinning, Don worked the gearshift, with a moment's maneuvering slipped into gear, and pulled away from the curb. He looked into the rearview mirror: a mask from which his eyes peered out. I waved.

Six or eight blocks down and more or less homeward, a battered Buick Regal pulled up, rocking, alongside me and a man leapt out from the driver's seat. Sweat poured off him. He shook.

"Can you help me, man? My wife's having a baby."

I bent down to look through a back window permanently at half mast with a square of cardboard bracing it in place, floor an undergrowth of fast-food wrappers and sacks, throwaway cups with lids and straws still in them, beer cans. Terrified round eyes peered back out at me.

"I came home from work and found her like this," he said. "I don't think we're gonna make it to the hospital. Something's wrong."

"Help me," she said. "Please. It hurts. Hurts bad."

She was white. Might be well along in the race's evolution, but it was still the South. I knew what could happen if I got in the back of that car.

Moments later, I had a different kind of trouble from the kind I'd anticipated.

Back in Paris, Vicky worked as an OB nurse. She'd told me about those years, how dullingly routine the work was mostly, how reaffirming it could be occasionally, how horrible it might suddenly turn without warning. I knew enough to recognize a bad delivery. Contractions were strong but the baby didn't seem to

228 ◆ JAMES SALLIS

be moving along the birth canal. I thought I saw something up there, a head, a shoulder, but couldn't be sure. My mind ground and spun like Don's transmission, searching Vicky's stories for the appropriate word.

Breech.

"It's going to be all right," I told her. "Don't be afraid." I was sufficiently afraid for us all.

Pain goosestepped over her face as the puppeteer worked fingers and strings. She clamped down on directives of pain just long enough to meet my eyes. She nodded. Then another wave hit and she passed out.

I stood bent over, half in and half out of the car, thinking of Deborah's earrings: mouthdown sharks swallowing swimmers. I was in way over my head. As was this child.

Knuckles rapped on the window. I backed out expecting the husband and father. Police. Cavalry. Please.

"You got a license for that, boy?"

Doc stood there looking in, cup of coffee in his hand. Streaks of brown down the side where it'd spilled from his tremors. Layers of clothing, greasy thin hair, traces of this morning's fast food, possibly yesterday's, in his beard.

I shook my head.

"Neither do I," he said. "Used to, though. Looks like you all could use some help."

I told him what I thought. He nodded, considering.

"You're probly right. K&B right across the street there. Get me a bottle of rubbing alcohol, whatever's the cheapest."

"But—"

"Now," he said.

When I returned, he took the bottle from me,

poured its contents carefully over his hands, and wiped them on his shirttail. "Do what we can," he said as he ducked into the backseat.

"Okay, she's fully dilated . . . I see . . . Not the head, though . . . You're right, it's a breech . . . And the cord's . . . Damn . . . Ain't seen this for a long time . . . If I can't . . . Can't seem to . . . Wait, I think . . . Okay, I've got it . . . You're gonna be fine, honey . . . Yeah, I do . . . Almost there, ma'am . . . Sorry if I was a little rough . . . It's a boy."

Enveloped with mucus, smeared with blood, the newborn lay nestled in Doc's arms. He held it out to me, and as he did, the tremors, which had stopped when he bent over the young woman, started up again. Hands trembling, he tore strips of cloth from the woman's slip and tied off the cord, cut between ties with a pocket knife. Tears streamed down his face.

"You never quite get over it," he said.

When I went in for the alcohol, I'd asked the store clerk to call an ambulance, which now arrived.

"Heart rate's 160 or thereabouts," Doc told the paramedics. "Color good, good capillary fill, good cry. Apgar, I'd put at about 9/9."

"You a doctor, sir?" one of them, a stocky woman of thirty or so with flyaway blond hair, name tag *Cherenski*, asked.

"Me? No, I'm a drunk. Speaking of which, I sure could use one right now. A drink, that is."

Shaking her head, Cherenski set to work, checking vitals, wrapping the baby in sterile batting, starting IVs.

"You did good here, sir," she told Doc.

"Let's get that drink," I said.

We found a bar half a block down, where Doc sat beside me through four double whiskeys. His tears never let up the whole time, and I made no effort to talk. When we parted outside he nodded thanks, starting off in one direction then abruptly reversing. I don't suppose it made much difference, finally.

Drop by drop at the heart, the pain of the pain remembered comes again, Aeschylus wrote in *Agamemnon.*

It sure as hell does. And the gods did no better than we've done ourselves. They never knew how to care for us, either.

32

AFTER a while I got up and walked to the window. I felt that if I didn't say anything, if I didn't think about what had happened, didn't acknowledge it, somehow it might all be all right again. I listened to the sound of my feet on the floor, the sounds of cars and delivery vans outside, my own breath. Whatever feelings I had, had been squeezed from me. I was empty as a shoe. Empty as the body on the bed behind me.

A limb bowed and pecked at the window, bowed and pecked again. Winds were coming in across Lake Ponchartrain with pullcarts of rain in their wake. I heard music from far off but couldn't tell what it was, not even what kind. Maybe only wind caught in the building's hard throats and hollows, or the city's random noise congealing.

Sooner or later I'd have to move. Go back out there, into the world, a world much smaller now, where it was about to rain. And where one of the coldest winters in New Orleans history like a bit player waited impatiently in the wings, strutting and thrumming, for its cue to go on.

Out there in the window-world where a moth beat against glass, a man I knew both too well and not at all stood watching. A man dark and ill-defined, with the mark of lateness, of the autumnal, upon him too.

I must come to some sort of conclusion, I suppose, I had written, years ago. *I can't imagine what it should be.*

Now I knew.

33

THIS is what happened, this is the truth.

Drop by drop at the heart, the pain of the pain remembered comes again. Memory holds you down while regret and sorrow kick hell out of you. Minutes drop like black cherries from my side.

A birth, a death. Just the kind of balance and open structure my father always loved. He got off the streets finally, though never as far as he thought he had, or as far as he wanted. Nor did he ever, quite, get away from drinking. In those last years it didn't ride him as it had, didn't rent out the front room like before, but it was still a frequent and welcome visitor. Many nights, as levels of Scotch or wine fell in their bottles, he'd talk about books he loved, books he wanted to write. So I guess part of what I'm doing is writing them for him. Five so far; this, I think, the last.

David here, if you've not yet realized it.

Books and women, his friends, had saved him, he

said. And then he would quote Blake. *The Imagination is not a State: it is the Human Existence itself.*

Four years ago now that he died.

Four years since, on a bleary six-o'clock morn, so hot already that sweat was pooling in hollows of chest and back, I came to the end of that first book and wrote the words, *a man I know both very well and not at all.* My father was a complicated man, self-educated and bizarrely ignorant of whole swaths of knowledge yet the best-read person I ever met, gentle with those he loved, violent with others and with himself, a man who often seemed to be pursuing redemption with one hand, self-destruction with the other. I know I'll never understand my father's life. He came up in a world I can only imagine. Most of all, I think, I treasure that single picture of him sitting with his own father on the steps by the train station as they ate their pass-through breakfasts and Grandfather spoke of invisible men. One of many stories he told me. Like others, I urged him to write them down, but he never did.

We can never truly know others, of course. We're condemned without pardon to our own lives and minds, these islands of self. No one believed that more than my father. And no one believed it more important that we keep trying to break through, to break out—even knowing all the time we can't.

In having that last chance to get to know him, I was blessed. I'm not sure we ever spoke of much of anything substantial, but speak we did, for hours, sitting at the kitchen table, in the living room looking out those tall windows, on the gallery steps over coffee, beers, whatever he was drinking at the time, my iced tea. He'd been a stranger to me for most of my life. Only in those last years did I come, as much as I ever will, to know him. Not an easy time for either of us. When, overwhelmed and confused, waking each morning with terrors I think he knew all too well, I fled, he risked everything he had to find me. There at the end it was Don who came. Following up with Greevy, the forensic entomologist, he learned where the body they'd first thought mine had come from. Don stepped up to me one day outside a Circle K across the river in Algiers to tell me my father was dying.

Finally it doesn't much matter what's true here, what imagined. In trying to re-create my father, I've used whatever sleights and subterfuges seemed to work. The life he lived in the mind was every bit as important to him and as real as, often more so than, the one he lived externally. He loved old blues, the flatness and predictability and emotional charge of them, things like "Po' Boy, Long Way from Home," "Going Back to Florida," "Death Letter Blues." And he loved improvisation, Sidney Bechet, Eric Dolphy, Charlie Parker, Monk, Lester Young, those unexpected back-flips, self-crossings and contradictions. There at the end oddly enough, Alouette tells me, it wasn't these he listened to, but Bob Dylan's "Knockin' on Heaven's Door," playing it over and over.

Please take these chains off of me, I can't use them anymore.

Deborah found him on the floor in the hall. She'd called back to see if they could have dinner before the play and, getting no answer, not even the machine, grew worried. Five tries later, she had Willie drive her over. Still had her key. Almost immediately after speaking to her and hanging up the phone my father had suffered another stroke, not a small one this time. He'd been unconscious, how long he had no idea, and, since, had been trying to drag himself back to the phone, but the right side of his body had seceded. Whole damn thing (he said weeks later, laughing) went south.

God, how I remember his laugh.

Here's what else Alouette tells me:

He wasn't able to do much there towards the end. I'd help him down to the park, or he'd sit on the porch for hours with a blanket, watching people come and go. Once every week or so he'd try to make dinner and I'd pretend to eat it. Most nights, I'd read to him.

He'd adopted a pigeon. Marvin. First took to Marvin because he was apart from the rest. Something was wrong with the bird—its beak was misshapen, it hobbled when it walked, dipped when it flew. Lew'd go clambering out into the backyard whenever Marvin showed up, to put out food. He'd run off all the others; after a while Marvin learned it was okay, he could stay. One afternoon Lew found Marvin in the bag of feed. He'd got in there and it was so cramped he couldn't get back out. Lew tipped the bag over and he walked on out. I don't know how many times your father told me that story.

He always knew Marvin wasn't long for this world. And over a space of weeks he watched him go down, feeding him, putting out water, talking to him the whole time. Last few days, Marvin couldn't even get to the dish. Lew'd take it out to him and stand there while he ate, keeping the others away.

Then one morning Marvin didn't come. Lew spent most of two days out there in the yard waiting, watching. And when he finally gave up and came in, it was as though it was all over for him, nothing else was left.

Your father went to bed. The next morning I took his coffee in and couldn't rouse him. He wouldn't speak to me. I'm not sure he could even see anymore. He turned his face to the wall. You know the rest.

There's precious little. Though in a sense at least my father's life goes on in these books, just as did all those lives he lived in his mind.

Midnight as I write this final page. I just walked out on the porch. Clouds are coming in fast over the lake, butting their blunt, dumb heads at dark sky. Soon it will be raining. He always loved storms, I remember.

I miss you, Lew.